Wendy Lewis is the best-selling author of *See Australia and Die*. She has written 11 books specialising in true crime and also writes for stage and musical theatre. For more info: www.wendylewiswriter.com

Please Forgive us, Richard Hauptmann

Wendy Lewis

Publishing services provided by Critical Mass
www.critmassconsulting.com

For my mother
In memory of my father and my brother

With lots of love

Contents

Death By Steps: Beware the Houses — 2
Giving up Spray Painting Means Less Expenditure — 14
Moluccan Cockatoo — 26
My Sister-in-Law the Fish — 38
The Other Place — 46
The White Cat — 56
But I Miss it — 64
Dusty Springfield's Voice — 82
Vale David McComb — 88
Three Poems — 92
Do Not Touch — 96
SPOTTED — 102
One Syllable Beginning with 'S' — 114
Ned Kelly, Ex-Bushranger — 126
The Frozen — 130
And Santo Took to the Sky — 134
Not Lauderdale Avenue — 146
Please forgive us, Richard Hauptmann — 156
Death by Realisation: The Philosopher's Sister Goes to South America — 178
burnt: fire to ash in five acts — 186
The Rocket, The Tea towel and The Lover — 192
The Motel with No Doors — 202

I lived briefly in Wellington in the late 1990's. It was a friendly, human-scale city. Peak hour was non-existent. The people were lovely and generous. And everyone was called Martin or Raewyn. Sitting in a sunny little wooden flat in Norna Crescent, I wrote a lot of short stories during this period, all inspired in one way or another by living in New Zealand. Wellington was very steep and very windy. This story captures the steepness.

Death By Steps: Beware the Houses

In retaliation for his ongoing interference with their enquiries into the disappearance of his sister, the police sent Steve to New Zealand. Not just anywhere in New Zealand. Wellington. And he couldn't just live in Wellington. He couldn't put his feet up and enjoy a break or put his feet down and partake in delightful treks in the forest. No. They arranged a job for him as a removalist.

It is not usual for police to line up employment for relatives of missing persons.

'Just to teach him a lesson. That bloke really irritates me,' said Superintendent Phillips as Steve left the inner Sydney police station after another typically unfruitful discussion about the whereabouts of Zoe. He didn't know why Steve got on his nerves so much.

There was nothing particularly unlikeable about the friendly-good-looking-average-height-average-weight young man who had just left the station but Superintendent Phillips couldn't help but find him a little hard to take

'His latest theory,' Superintendent Phillips told a bored colleague who was tucking into a giant slice of four seasons pizza, 'is that his sister must have been kidnapped by a semi-ludicrous cult led by a German veterinarian called Sigmund who are planning to fling themselves into the crater of Mt Ruapeho at the next full moon.'

'A war veteran?'

'A veterinarian. A vet. Woof. Woof. Meow.'

'Mt Ruapeho?'

'It's a volcano.'

'In Melbourne? Sigmund as in Freud?'

'Sigmund as in...er...' Phillips flicked over his notebook, 'O'Leary.' He let the Melbourne reference go by.

'When's the next full moon?' asked the Superintendent's colleague doggedly, but Phillips wasn't listening which is just as well. He was on the phone, doing a deal with his cousin who ran a furniture removal company in Wellington. Well, a cousin-in-law really.

When the police approached Steve with the whole package deal: job offer, airline ticket, accommodation, all expenses paid, the idea appealed to him immediately. (The ticket was one way, but at that stage it didn't arouse his suspicions.) He thanked Phillips profusely for giving him the opportunity to examine the scene of the crime at first hand. Wellington, you see, was where Zoe was last seen.

Superintendent Phillips was glad to wipe his hands of the case – he'd done all he could at his end – which was basically to establish that since Steve's sister had disappeared in New Zealand it wasn't his problem. And even though Phillips was a professional and did not let personal likes and dislikes influence his judgement in police cases, he really didn't like Steve.

The police sniggered as they discussed travel arrangements with Steve which unnerved him slightly. It crossed his mind that spontaneously offering plane flights and job offers to relatives of missing persons was odd but any reservations he had at taking up their kind offer were washed away by the excitement he felt at the opportunity to do his own super-sleuthing once he got over there. He would find his sister, he would do it. And as for being a furniture removalist, the work would be strenuous, yes. A little out-of-left-field, yes. But nothing he couldn't handle.

No, Steve. No, no, Steve. Don't do it.

Wellington is made up of a series of winding roads that circumnavigate the hills circling the city centre. Tucked behind the roads, hidden away behind neat pines and walls of daisies are the houses. Hardly any of them are on street level. They are either built below the road or rise up reached by I'll-build-a-stairway-to-Paradise staircases. No, staircase is not the right word. Steps. Pure and simple steps. Dozens of them. Tens of thousands of them. At least fifty or sixty steps up to each house.

Steve whistled in amazement when it began to dawn on him what life in Wellington would be like. He calculated how many steps he would be negotiating on a daily basis. And the more he thought about it, the more he didn't like it. And when he added the weight of various pieces of furniture to his calculations (piano X kgs, bookcase Y kgs, double bed + mattress Z kgs) and figured out that he would often have to carry the load up the slope, not down, he became rather disheartened at the thought of starting his shiny new job. Still, he would give it a go, because that's the kind of man he was – positive and likeable to basically everyone except Superintendent Phillips.

He owed it to his sister Zoe. He had to get amongst the New Zealanders, get to know how their minds work and maybe he would glean valuable information. It did not once occur to him that the whole Wellington set-up was thanks to Superintendent Phillips' unique blend of personal concern and malice, cleverly designed to destroy.

From the start Steve had problems adjusting to the lifestyle of this strange topographically arranged city. You cannot survive in Wellington without being in peak physical condition because if you are not, you cannot reach your house every evening when you come home from work. That is not strictly true. You can reach the house. But unless you have a will of steel, you cannot find the energy to hoist yourself up the last few steps to get to the front door.

Steve did not know it yet but Wellington is unkind to visitors who do not play by the rules. He did not know that if only his sister had been a little more careful, she may still have been alive today. But she was dead, as dead as a shrivelled up daisy bush in February.

Yes, Steve. Yes, yes, Steve. Don't think about it.

It was only slowly that the full horror of his idyllic stay in this picturesque city of hills came to him. In glimpses, in whisperings behind gorse hedges, in the absence of elderly ladies with shopping trolleys which was such a familiar sight in his home country. Where do the old people go? he thought. They must be shipped off to flatter places...I mean, they wouldn't dispose of them, would they?

Yes, Steve. Yes, yes, Steve. Don't think about it.

He soon discovered that everyone jogged in Wellington, yet another subtle reminder of the tell-tale absence of aged and/or incapacitated residents. At any time of day or night, the pound of fluoro sport shoes would float up to where Steve sat contemplating

Zoe's unsolved fate and indeed, his own. Thud, thud, thud…thud, thud, thud…yet another Wellingtonian in training for their day-to-day existence. Yet another Wellingtonian making sure they would not be left by the wayside, just out of reach of the safety and warmth of their beloved home. Because it seemed to Steve that they had a fear of being left. A terror of not getting there. A great trepidation of not making it up the steps to their house. And in thinking this, Steve was perfectly correct.

It is not unusual for physically unfit Wellingtonians to 'disappear.'

There are many small white wooden crucifixes scattered through New Zealand, particularly on Motorway 2 out of Wellington through Lower Hutt. New arrivals, like Steve, believe they are commemorating loss of life through traffic accidents, but no, they mark the spots where hapless New Zealanders have collapsed, unable to cry for help, just out of reach of their houses. All is safe in the houses, if only they could reach them. Conversely, outside the houses…

It is not usual for Wellingtonians to discuss these things.

There is a telephone number in the Wellington White pages for anyone who has come within reach of their house but is unable to make it up the steps. The number offers friendly advice at 99c a minute

(GST included). This is a number rarely used – it is the Number of Shame – and no Wellingtonian would be seen dead dialling the helpline for two reasons. Firstly, it indicates that you have failed at negotiating steps, one of the fundamentals of Wellington living, and you are thereby regarded with thinly veiled condemnation as a pathetic creature unworthy of the necessities of life such as food, water, lycra and companionship. The second reason why Wellingtonians never dial the Number of Shame is fate. People who use this number are ostracised, excommunicated, or worse.

New Zealanders know what happens when the 'friendly' operator takes your call and foreigners do not.

'Norna Crescent.'

'Nearest cross street, ma'm?'

'Raroa Road.'

'Number of steps to be negotiated?'

'Sixty two.'

'Next of kin living in New Zealand?'

'Pardon?'

'Next of kin living in New Zealand?'

'What's that got to do with –?'

'Do you have relatives here?'

'No.'

A pause. Slight but eerily ominous.

'No rellies? We'll be right there.'

Breathing a sigh of relief, she puts her mobile phone away. Suddenly, a blaze of light, a siren excruciatingly loud…unidentifiable noises, a crowd of people who weren't there before, the rush of wind, more strange sounds, a shout, a cry, a scream, no, no, no…and then…nothing.

A small white cross appears in Norna Crescent. When the police later try to trace the whereabouts of Ms Australian Tourist they reach a dead end. There is no record of her last call. Strange. The police shake their heads. They say nothing and go back to setting speed traps on the Desert Road.

It is not unusual for Wellingtonian police to shake their heads.

Did Steve's sister dial the Number of Shame? Yes, she did. Was the above an accurate transcript of her final telephone conversation? No, it wasn't. It was severely edited. Zoe dialled the Number of Shame even though she was a fit young woman, fully capable of running up stairs, indeed she could run up stairs while juggling three oranges, adding up $\sqrt{(6 \times 16.264)}$ and carrying out a simple conversation in Swahili at beginner's level. She had finely honed aerobic and endurance skills and was not someone who would collapse by the wayside, calling for help, unable to go further.

What could possibly have induced her to dial the Number of Shame?

If the police had been a little more forthcoming in their investigation, they could have told Steve that the last number she had attempted to dial on her mobile was for pizza. They found a small glossy flyer with a picture of a steaming hot possum and mushroom pizza near the scene of her disappearance and surmised that she had misdialled the second digit and, consequently, had been connected to the Number of Shame.

The Wellington police did not inform Steve of this development because they feared he would ask too many questions. And so he was left with a mind full of doubts, the possibility that he would never know what happened to Zoe, and his sister's mobile phone. (The police did the courtesy of returning it to him with the last number dialled erased and tell-tale signs of mozzarella removed).

Steve is troubled. Why have they sent me here if they don't want my help and they don't answer my questions? This city where everything seems nice but nothing seems right? I'll make it, he tells himself, doing a passable impression of the positive thinking that had recently deserted him. I'll find out what happened to Zoe. I won't be afraid of first impressions, rumours, that certain something in the air, what other people say. But he must confess to a certain uneasiness, a certain distrust of his fellow human beings…

No, Steve. No, no, Steve. Don't do it.

'Time for your first day on the job,' smiles Kai, the hefty New Zealander who'll be showing Steve the ropes. This is Superintendent Phillips' cousin – well, cousin-in-law – and he is happy to do him a 'favour' as they say in the force.

Steve leaps into the back of the furniture removal truck and Kai slides the door shut behind him. Steve hears the sound of a key being turned. Kai has dead-locked the back of the truck. Superintendent Phillips' cousin-in-law jumps into the driver's seat, revs the engine, turns round and beams at Steve as the truck pulls out of the depot and heads towards the houses.

I have always loved weatherboard cottages. And California bungalows. And Federation houses. Not to mention Art Deco in all its shapes and forms and Art Nouveau, not that there's much of that in Australia. Sydney, the city where I live, grows more and more nightmarish with its obsession with 'knock-downs', project homes and rendering every façade in sight. Will grey go out of fashion soon, please? I had a short stay in Melbourne recently and found myself in a Southbank tower with floor-to-ceiling glass staring down at the city lights like the boy in the story and thinking that being so high is weird.

Giving up Spray Painting Means Less Expenditure

There was an eight-year-old boy with dark curly hair and angry eyes. They were a wild, uncanny blue, blazing to cobalt when he was angry and shrinking to violet when he was sad. He lived in an apparently exclusive apartment on the thirty-second floor overlooking the only park in the city.

His apartment had floor-to-ceiling glass which in the old days was called giant picture windows because views were important. But now it was called floor-to-ceiling glass because interiors and finishes were most important of all. It was essential to have dove grey feature walls, a stainless-steel refrigerator that said 'hello' when you opened it and a private helipad.

He stood staring down at the messy patchwork of palm trees and pansies, the joggers criss-crossing the trampled buffalo grass and the ibises perched on overflowing garbage bins with transparent sides. A multitude of cars attempted to leave the city as they stop-start-stop-started around the four sides of the highly regular but slowly dying open space.

The front door lock turned but the boy didn't.

'Take your hands off the glass.'

'Why are we so high?' he asked his mother, still gazing down as the sun spread its last weak streaks of orange across the sky and removing his sticky palms from the window at the last possible moment.

'It's the latest,' she smiled as she flicked off her killer stiletto heels and padded into the kitchen to prepare quinoa salad with grapefruit for her and cheese toasties for the kids.

* * *

The boy's sister was different.

Every Wednesday afternoon he and his sister visited their grandma who lived in a neat yellow weatherboard cottage that took thirty minutes by car. His mother used to sigh a lot when they went. He used to think it was because it was a long way to drive. Then he thought it was because his mother didn't really want to visit her mother on her one day off although she pretended she did. Then he changed his mind. His mother often sighed.

He loved to stare out the window of the car as it stop-start-stop-started its way through roundabouts and stop signs and no left turns. He saw cigarette butts in gutters and strange liquid stains on the stairs of office blocks and adults in dark clothes pacing up and down, talking to themselves. But after a while he saw an ornate metal fence in the shape of grevillea and stained glass windows the colour of rosellas and golden Art Deco lettering on old shops. And as the final fingers of the city groaned and slowly ran out of space, he saw little cottages with giant sunflowers, gardening shops with rambling honeysuckle vines and homes that welcomed him.

He loved his grandma's house and garden. He watched butterflies. And every twenty minutes a red rattler would go by the back fence, making all the pot plants shake.

His sister was bored.

'There's nothing to do,' she said. She sighed just like her mother and sat in a slump on the verandah with her chin in her hands, hoping someone would come and rescue her from this terrible suburban boredom.

Another rattling old train went by.

That night Grandma died and left the house to his mother.

His mother decided to sell.

'You can't do that,' he sobbed.

'Stupid old house,' said his sister.

His mother looked blankly at her two children and then out of the floor-to-ceiling glass, frowning at the smudged palm prints. Damn incompetent cleaner.

'You're right,' she said. 'I'll demolish the house, rebuild and sell.'

Nooooo.

The boy ran into his room, slammed the door, and lay on his bed, sobbing.

* * *

The boy is no longer a boy. He catches the train to his sound engineering course. He grows a beard of sorts, wears tight leather and has a stud in his tongue. He has chosen a career that he has no interest in. He would rather study butterflies.

He finds the course demanding. Obscure. He doesn't like it but he catches the train obediently every morning and looks out the window without thinking too hard. His eyes flicker at the rusty old ornate metal fence in the shape of grevillea. But the stained glass windows and Art Deco letters are gone. Sticky purple lantana has strangled the giant sunflowers. The backyard of his grandma's house is now a giant hole in the ground hemmed in by scaffolding.

He hates everything. He spray paints fences. He smashes windows of derelict houses.

His mother is embarrassed. And angry. He waits for her to say what she always says: 'I've given up a lot for you.'

He begins smashing windows in residential streets. Double-storey family homes with swimming pools. He doesn't care. He destroys letter boxes with metal poles and scrawls obscene slogans on driveways in fat blue chalk. He starts breaking into garages and entering houses via internal doors. He smashes IKEA tables and bookshelves made of MDF, throws blenders onto kitchen floors and tramples them with his black boots. He hates the things that people have.

His sister disowns him.

'You're a destructive idiot,' she tells him. She leaves home and moves into a trendy apartment just down the road from their mother's apartment. She shares it with two other giggling 17-year-old girls. She is naïve and young-looking but clever enough to study Architecture at university. She doesn't like it and switches in third year to Town planning. She has found what she wants. She excels and wins the University medal. She has so many plans and ideas and ambitious schemes. But no dreams. She never dreams.

And she never looks out train windows.

* * *

Three days after his mother kicks him out he gets thrown into jail for being a destructive idiot. In jail he reads books about the history of tea and moths of Africa and old things and times past and the ticking of clocks. He stares through the bars but there's nothing to see. He considers stabbing his eyes out with a fork but he's too scared to try. Every morning he doesn't want to leave his cell for exercise but the wardens make him. His mother comes to see him once. She stares at him like he is a Blue Triangle pinned to a sheet of cardboard. She looks blankly at the stained walls.

'That window is very small,' she sniffs.

This does not suit her image. He is supposed to be an asset not a liability. She does not visit again.

That night he has a dream. His grandma asks him to go back to her house and make sure it's all right.

'Look,' she says and shows him an old piece of weatherboard with peeling pale green paint.

'We wanted the house to be sea foam green but –' She shrugs. 'Times were tough and the hardware store had a special on downy duck yellow so Grandpa and I –'

She shrugs again and smiles at him. 'Bloody downy duck yellow.'

'It's all right, Grandma,' he says.

When he wakes up he is smiling.

* * *

Three days later he is released from jail. He catches the train to his grandma's house and walks along a much changed street where garden gnomes rub shoulders with $350 Yuccas in $350 pots. There is a brand new almost complete residential tower rising into the sky. His sister is there, all smiles, dressed like a high-class escort, exchanging words with some kind of real estate monster.

Nooooo.

He rushes at her.

'Did you do this?' he yells. She is a town planner, he thinks. She destroys things. She knocks them down. She is full of hate.

She gives the real estate monster an I-can-handle-this smile and looks him up and down. 'So they let you out?'

'Did you?' he shouts.

She rolls her eyes.

'No, you destructive idiot. I do useful work. Unlike some people. I plan, I design, I predict. I study movement, residents, expectations, traffic flow, sustainability, marketability, landscaping…'

He puts his hands over his ears. She doesn't know anything about how to live well, he thinks. She wouldn't know a beautiful home if she fell over one. He unblocks his ears and she is still talking.

'…I didn't make the decisions about the land use of this subdivision,' she said. 'I don't work on a domestic scale. But I do like this. That's why I'm buying one.'

She waves official looking papers under his nose. She is signing the contract to buy the penthouse on the block of land that the yellow weatherboard house his grandma owned used to be.

He sees red.

He bursts through the OPENING SOON signs and pushes his way into the deathly white marble foyer. The real estate monster shouts out and sprints after him but is too late to stop him getting into the lift. It is not a tall block – the thirteenth floor is the top floor. He gets out swiftly, strides down the corridor and rams his fist into the walnut-panelled door of his sister's soon-to-be-purchased penthouse. The door gives way with a splintery crash as he flies into the living room, heading straight for the floor-to-ceiling glass. He runs at it like an enraged bull, bracing himself to smash through the glass and plunge to his death on the railway line below.

He crumples onto the mahogany floors in a concussed heap.

It is safety glass.

* * *

Crowds gathered at the site of this singularly heartfelt act of sacrifice. Newspapers, radio and TV buzzed with news of the passionate young man and his act of protest. What did this young man want? Why did he do it? Was he making a statement?

From his hospital bed he said 'No'.

Offers came in from all over the country. Ordinary people saw in him a sanity that seemed irreconcilable with running headfirst into a window. A mildness of spirit. A rare urban wisdom. They admired him without knowing why. High flyers saw in him potential to make money.

'We want you in our splashy ad campaign about how important it is to preserve neat yellow weatherboard cottages,' they told him.

'Really?' he said.

'Actually, we're more interested in having nice long lunches at Shunawashimoyo's and then popping into that Thai massage place up the road, you know the one?'

'Have you considered giving lectures about the importance of heritage preservation?' asked a mournful academic with thinning hair.

'Not really.'

'We don't have the funding anyway,' said the academic.

A hearty builder with a greasy handshake slapped him on the back.

'This is what we'll do,' he said. 'Buy up all the weatherboard houses we can find and make sure no one ever gets their hands on them again.'

'Really?' he said, feeling hopeful for the first time in five years.

The developer laughed. 'You gotta be kidding, mate. Knock down, rebuild. Are you crazy or what?'

* * *

Strangely, the conversation stayed with him. He withdrew from his sound engineering course.

Every day he searched and searched but he never found it.

He became a volunteer at the zoo working in the aviary, marvelling at the blue grey feathers of the Victorian crowned pigeon. Two months later he got a part-time job at a butterfly farm and decided the ornate dusk-flat was his favourite. He found that giving up spray painting obscene slogans meant less expenditure and less angst. He started saving money.

Every day he searched and searched but he never found it.

Until one day. It was a long way away. Almost four hours from his mother's apartment. And three and half hours from where his grandma's house used to be. He bought a neat weatherboard cottage in a small dying country town and painted it sea foam green. And every night he waited for his grandma to come to him so that he could tell her it was all right.

Environmental vandalism, domestic homicide, kid-napping...crime comes in many shapes and forms. And then there's the lesser publicised crime of wildlife smuggling. Yellow crested cockatoos stuffed in mineral water bottles. A drugged rhesus monkey hidden under the blouse of a young woman who pretends to be pregnant. Even tiger cubs, frozen and wrapped in plastic, who may or may not survive the trip. Such a despicable, opportunistic crime.

Moluccan Cockatoo

Disgusting. The smell of eggs. There is nothing worse than being force-fed egg sandwiches. Even the word makes me sick. My mother did it to me all the time. I think it was the only thing she could cook. But I'm a big girl now and I've cut off that part of my life.

These days when we have spare cash, I ask Grinder whether we can go out for breakfast. He thinks cafés are stupid. But sometimes he'll let me. We'll sit on milk crates next to the main road in the shadow of the expressway and check out the menu. Poached eggs. Why the hell does everything for breakfast come with a bloody poached egg? You can even get a side order. Smashed avo with poached egg plus poached egg. Bonus. I will never eat another egg in my life.

It started off with simple things. Like Salami. Easy. As long as the sniffer dogs weren't around. I would declare something benign like a block of chocolate and they would confiscate it and wave me through.

And he would give me money.

Not much but enough to keep me hanging on. Then he wanted more.

'I'm not risking my neck,' I said, 'no drugs.'

He agreed. Moved up into the art world. First a few inexpensive pieces stolen from some gallery somewhere. And then we ramped it up a bit. Some were pricey. An etching. A sketch. A print from some whacko photographer who liked severed body parts.

Then I advanced to more three dimensional pieces. A statue of some fertility goddess. I carried it on – and off – the plane. They didn't catch me. Art? Pish posh. Another statue. He said it was 900 years old. That can't be right. Maybe it was nine years old. Always small and easy to hide.

My bank account was creeping up. I had a healthy sense of self esteem. More confidence than ever before. Well, that wasn't hard given my childhood. Mustn't get carried away. But we were onto a good thing. And I liked him. More than liked him. Do anything for him.

Weird things like a dried head.

'Human, that's right,' he said. 'A mate wants to practice voodoo.'

Well, yes, I supposed. Just as long as the head's original owner hadn't been surprised when it was detached from his spinal cord.

'A natural death,' he assured me, grinning at me with a gap where his front tooth and incisor used to be.

'No worries. Any health issues? I mean, dead body parts? A bit bacterial.'

'It's been sprayed,' he said. 'You could eat your dinner off it.'

'Funny,' I said. 'Where would you put your knife and fork?'

He put his hand up my dress.

'Wanna fork?' he said.

No, he didn't. He doesn't know what a pun is.

I was good. Good at not being nervous. Good at knowing when to meet the eyes of the custom official and when to be coy. I was good at looking vulnerable.

I've never been good at much but I was good at this.

Sometimes I took my two-year-old with me – not his, mine – to look family-oriented. I'd make up a bullshit story about my husband being in the navy and I missed him so much and I'd get teary if I thought it would get me through the gates. Sometimes I'd maintain my poise and be Little Miss Self-Control. Haughty. Mysterious. Once the Customs guy gave me the eye. We went back to a little room he knew and we fucked on the floor and I kept sneezing because of the dust and I'm glad I remembered to take off my undies with the Umbrella cockatoo eggs sewn inside before he got into it or it could have been revelatory.

Rare birds' eggs. Huh, eggs have come back to haunt me. I don't want to touch them but he talks me into it.

'Eggs is just eggs,' he says. 'You don't have to cook them. They just sit there doing nothing.'

After the Umbrella cockatoo episode, I brought in some African Greys in specially made plastic bags strapped to my legs. Then I brought in some eggs from a Moluccan cockatoo in my stockings. With a bit of padding round the ankles.

He's pleased with me. One of those birds is worth thousands. Whoa. How many mugs are out there willing to pay megabucks for the privilege of owning a pretty birdy? You'd be surprised.

I start educating myself. I dig out this big book of birds with colour photos. It's cool. First book I've looked at since I left school. I flick through it. Moluccan cockatoo...Moluccan cockatoo...the Moluccan cockatoo is a threatened species. Could die out. Bringing them into the country is an offence under the Environment Protection and Biodiversity Conservation Act 1999. See, I know my stuff.

I need to convince myself I'm doing nothing wrong.

Very intelligent bird. Gorgeous peachy pink. Loves to scream for the hell of it. Endangered? Well, let some lucky bugger look after it, cherish it.

* * *

'Let's get creative,' he says. He wheels out a wheelchair. 'You can be like those – what do you call it? – Paralympians.'

'Nifty,' I say.

I'm learning things all the time.

Getting me through the doors and onboard the plane is a hoot. So much attention taken up with my wheelchair. Airline staff treating me like a moron. And all the people on the plane staring at me when they realise that not looking at me is worse. I'm laughing inside.

The six little ember crested geckos I have in specially sewn bags wrapped around my waist have the time of their lives too. I can sort of feel them but they're not exactly speed demons. Pretty sluggish really.

I get through Customs at the other end, no probs. I wheel myself off to catch a taxi and stare out at the industrial wasteland. I'm careful to keep up the charade. The taxi driver is very considerate. I tell him all about winning a silver medal in cross-country skiing at the Paralympics in Chile and he believes me. Helps me with my bag. Wants to help me inside. I tell him I'm right.

I open the door.

'I'm home.'

'G'day,' he says, not looking up from the stupid mindless moronic zombie death bitch car crash game he's playing.

'Would be nice to have a bit of appreciation,' I say. 'Did you fix the tap?'

He doesn't say anything.

'I've just got thirty thousand bucks worth of bloody lizards into the country and you can't even say thank you, bastard.'

I snatch my money and go to the bedroom. He comes at me all smooth and sexy but I'm not buying it.

'Fuck off. I'm tired.'

'Sitting in a bloody wheelchair for six hours?'

'You try it.'

He grins and goes back to shooting people to hell. Rip rip rip go the lasers or the blasters or whatever the fuck they are. Later he slides in beside me in the dark, pulls me, twists me, jerks me like a game controller. Then he rolls over.

* * *

'Baby tiger? Are you kidding?'

'It's easy,' he says.

'They'll see it right away,' I say. 'They'll see it.'

'Nah.'

'Heat detection. They have technology, you fuck. To find heart beats. Of live animals. You know? You know that.'

'Nah.'

He bites me where it hurts.

'Get off me,' I say.

'They'll drug it,' he says. 'Lower its body temperature 'til li'l tiggy wiggy's almost freezing.'

We're lying on our backs on the bed. He spreads his arms out like he's a bloody eagle.

'Think of it as sleepy bye byes in the sky skies.'

Idiot.

'Do you want me in the wheelchair?'

'Nah.'

'Then what was all that about?'

'It was an experiment,' he says.

An experiment?

'It won't move. It won't make a peep. And just for special effect,' he says, 'we put in two stuffed baby tiger toys on either side. So if anyone looks, they'll see little baby toys. Yeah...'

Dream on.

'Think about it,' he says, putting his hand down my t-shirt, 'no pressure.'

He squeezes my left breast until it hurts, sucks me, mauls me, tears at me until I'm close to screaming and then shoves me over and climbs onboard.

No pressure.

* * *

Close call with the baby tiger.

They take me aside, ask what's in my luggage. It's heavy and they notice me struggling. They frisk me all over. And I mean all over. But they don't take it further.

He goes back to rare birds' eggs. I keep reading up about it. I start feeling bad. Some eggs break. Baby birds taken away from their mothers for some shit-head collector with cash.

I decide I've had enough. I've proved I'm smart. And a lot of other things that my mum and brother never ever thought I could be.

I have a beer.

I'm not an idiot. Need a career change. Never thought I'd have a career let alone a change of one. I'll work in a flower shop. I like the smell of flowers. And I like tulips. Pink ones. Or at a dentist's. Be a nurse without having to be qualified. Wear a tight white uniform. Meet a nice rich man with gold fillings who'll drill me in his spare time.

'I don't want to do this any more,' I tell him.

'Yes, you do.'

'No, I don't.'

'You're my best worker. You know the ropes. Don't know what I'd do without you.'

He tries to put his hand down my jeans. I don't let him. He gets me another beer. In a fancy glass. Fancy that. I drink it. He tries again.

'Fuck off,' I say.

I close the bedroom door.

'Can you count backwards from ten?' he says from the hallway.

'Course I can. Ten, nine, eight…'

I have a nice long sleep. I dream of peachy pink tulips.

* * *

'Good morning.'

I hear his voice from what seems like a long way away.

I open my eyes. He's at the bedroom door with a funny smile on his face.

'Got a present for you.'

I try to pull myself up in the bed. The sheet is drenched with blood.

'What the fuck have you done?'

I don't have my left leg. My leg is gone. He has cut off my leg.

I am insane with anger. I screech like hell. I am in hell. I lunge at him but I hit my head on the side of the bed and knock myself out.

When I come to I think it must have been a dream.

'Don't you want to see the surprise?'

'I thought this was the surprise,' I say slowly. 'This lack of leg.'

'I got you a fake one. Prosthetic. Hollow at the top, see? One more run.'

'One more run. Are you insane?'

One more run.

'In the hollow?'

'Yeah.'

In the hollow.

'I'm not doing it.'

'Yes, you are.'

'I'm not doing it.'

'Yes, you are.'

* * *

I get to Customs. I find a Security Officer. I tell her everything. I catch a taxi home.

I wheel inside. I will wheel inside forever.

He is waiting. He comes over to me and licks my face and puts his filthy paws on my hips. I shiver. Then I remove the 30 centimetre bowie knife I smuggled in and squelch it into his stomach. He screams.

I slice again. He is on the floor, writhing. I have the upper hand. I have the prosthetic limb. And he is incapable of standing.

I slash at his hip now. I will sever his upper leg from his lower leg. He is screeching for me to stop but I can't hear. I hack into his flesh. I hear iguanas hissing. And a Moluccan cockatoo squawking with fear. I cut more carefully now. Slice, slice, crunch. As if there is a little black perforated line running around his thigh saying 'cut me'. I hear squirrel monkeys squealing and blinded black bears screaming and an abandoned tiger cub crying real tears. I cut and hack and rip and rage until a nice police officer smashes down the door and pulls me off him just as his sartorius muscle hangs loose like dripping bloody egg yolk.

When I was little, I had a psycho-goldfish called Shenanigan that jumped out of its bowl twice. On both occasions, I scooped him up and put him back and he seemed unperturbed. Then he attacked his friend, a little Black Moor called Dudley, and tried to eat him so Dudley was moved to safer accommodation. My next two fish, Barak and Colby, lived happily together in a tank with a snail with no drama at all.

My Sister-in-Law the Fish

She approached life with cold, calculating greed.

'She stares,' said her trusty brother-in-law Glen.

'A lot of people stare,' said Glen's wife, Sonia.

'At me? She stares at me.'

'A lot of people stare at you.'

'She doesn't blink. She doesn't smile.'

'The more you smile at her, the more uncomfortable she feels. It's a vicious circle.'

'I smile because I'm approachable not because I… Bugger it. She is so…'

'Intimidating? Infuriating?'

'Emotionless.'

'Do you wonder why?' asked Sonia.

'Yes,' said Glen.

Sonia was pretty in a gossamer filtered kind of way. She liked *The Australian Women's Weekly, Who* and *Cosmo* in that order. She had a gentle nature, dabbled in water colour, and wore a lot of lemon yellow. Glen loved her to pieces. Her sister Cath was the opposite. Harsh, silent and steely. She despised fluffy white dogs, red roses and children. Glen and Sonia had two children. Cath sent them money every year which Glen took as an admission that she couldn't remember how old they were, couldn't be bothered setting foot in a toy shop, or both.

Cath had no financial need to work, purely a psychological need to ruthlessly take on her opposition and win. Cath thought nothing of working all weekend and then popping up at the Monday morning meeting fresh as a daisy while her colleagues who had actually had a relaxing weekend more closely resembled bruised hibiscus petals trampled in wet sand.

Cath had no need for companionship, male or female, or holidays. She wrote down one foolscap page of New Year's Resolutions every year and kept them. She exercised virtuously, had a cellar full of the finest wines and an apartment that she had professionally re-styled every six months. One Wednesday night after returning home from her fourteen hour day at the office, she developed a strange red rash on her face and began to feel not in control.

She looked in the mirror and saw an ugly blotchy face. No light in her eyes, no colour on her lips. A dead fish face.

She began to cry. She cried until her apartment flooded and she ruined her $68,000 Persian rug. The company report she was reading was smudged beyond recognition and the ink stained her fingers and left strange blots on her perfectly applied nail polish. Her genuine Biedermeier antique walnut bookcase full of twenty-first century design books groaned under the weight of her salty tears. She cried until her sides ached with the memory of things she never had. She cried until her perfect teeth started tingling. She cried until her contact lenses slipped from her eyes and plunged in a miniature waterfall torrent onto the floor.

She rose from the table, steadying herself on its polished surface, but slipped into the pool of tears. The tears began to absorb her like some kind of malignant acid until she feared she would shrink and disappear and no one would ever find her.

'Help!' she screamed, each flaying of her arms sending her further down into the rising tears.

'Help!'

A knock at the door.

'Cath? It's Glen.'

Her brother-in-law. The easy going good natured one who had given up a well-paid job to go part-time so he could spend more time with the kids. How she despised people like that.

'Cath? Sonia asked me to drop round this recipe book.'

'I can't get to the door,' she spluttered.

'What?'

'Open the door!'

She tried to shout out with authority but her voice was strained and remote. Like a drowning creature finding a voice it never knew it had.

Glen smashed the door down and a wall of water swept past him down the stairs. He dog-paddled into the living room, looking in vain for his sister-in-law.

'Cath? Cath?' he shouted.

'Gle-heh-heh-hennnnn…' she wailed.

When Glen found her, he didn't know what to do. She had turned into a fish. A red spotted blenny. Istiblennius chrysospilos. A fish found off the coast of East Africa.

'Gle-heh-heh-hennnnn…'

She flopped into his arms, limp and pathetic, as if she had been caught on a line and flung into a tinny. He held her as gently as he could for fear that he would crush her.

'I'm sorry I have been such a bad sister-in-law. I'm sorry I hate your kids. I'm sorry I'm no fun.'

'There, there,' said Glen.

Cradling her gingerly, he swam across to the couch. It occurred to him on the way that, as she was now a fish, she was more at home in the water than he was. So why was he handling her this way? It seemed that she needed him and he was never one to withhold affection or attention when it was needed. Even if it was his sister-in-law.

He managed to drag one end of the couch out of the receding water and perched on it with Cath at his side, listlessly flapping.

He looked at her.

'Can you tell me what happened?'

She burst into tears.

'I've always loved you, Glen. You're warm and funny and you always ask me how I am even if you don't mean it and —'

'Cath, tell me what happened. Why are you a fish?'

'— you're nice to people,' she continued in her new high pitched voice. 'You eat sausages. And steak. I despise people who eat red meat. But you make it look so wholesome. You always enjoy yourself so much while you're doing it —'

'Cath —'

Cath swished her tail. It took them both by surprise.

'I don't want to be a fish!' she wailed.

'I'll ring Sonia.'

'No!' she said. 'Please don't. Let's work this out together.'

They sat in silence. Glen sat and Cath trod water.

'I've been cooking the books,' said Cath.

'What?'

'I've been doing it for months. It's so easy. The accountant is so uncreative.'

'I don't believe this —'

'I have access to everything. Today I transferred eighteen million to my account with a dodgy name. They won't be able to trace it, I'm positive. I'm going to skim some off the top because I deserve it but the rest I'm going to give to a girls' orphanage in Calcutta. Isn't Steve Waugh a saint? That's why I'm a fish.'

'Don't follow you, Cath.'

'God is punishing me.'

'God does not turn people into fish.'

'But he could.'

'I suppose…but, look, I do not see the hand of God in this.'

'I got away with it,' said Cath desperately. 'The nature of the Universe is such that you don't get away with things. I came home. Looked in the mirror. Felt hot with shame. Bingo. A red rash. It's a curse. A curse on me from all the accountants who have ever not fiddled the books. A curse on me from all the people who have ever been ripped off by smarmy people in suits. Not that I'm smarmy.' She looked at him feverishly. 'This red rash marks me as a monstrous woman. A hunted woman. I can't go out in public. People will think I have herpes. They will think I have a terrible, icky, you know…'

'Sexually transmitted disease,' said Glen in a loud, clear voice.

'Yes,' she whispered, mortified. 'Anyway,' she said suddenly sounding more like the Cath of Old, 'the thought of going to work tomorrow with facial skin like a leper is too much. It made me burst into tears.'

'So it wasn't the guilt?'

'What?'

'It wasn't the guilt that made you cry?'

'Nah.'

Glen thought long and hard for ten seconds. He waded into the kitchen and came back with a plastic bag. He popped Cath in the bag with sufficient oxygen for her to breathe. He felt like a little boy who has just bought a psycho-goldfish at the pet shop.

Back at home, he sat on the couch, holding the plastic bag, looking at Cath. He got the feeling that she was looking at him, searching for an answer, seeking assurance. He was waiting for Sonia to come home from her seafood cookery class. She was always in a good mood. Always enthusiastic to try something new.

Some people, thought Glen, some people are better off dead.

There's a *Tom and Jerry* episode where Tom is crushed to death by a piano but refused entry to Cat Heaven because he has spent his life persecuting a poor little mouse. His fate is to go to the Other Place where Spike the American Bulldog and a bubbling cauldron of eternal torment await. The gates of heaven is a wonderful setting for anything, be it an animation, a tortured piece of epic theatre or a simple short story.

The Other Place

Everything is white. Just like the clichés and poetic visions imagine it to be. Giant fluffy clouds, gleaming gowns and a sense of celestial well-being that just wouldn't cut it if it was dark and brooding.

God sits on his shiny throne with the List of Sins, surrounded by a throng of sinners who are to be held accountable for what they have done. Top of the List, A for adultery, the one everybody's waiting for, even the angels, those celestial beings without bodies. For sexless or rather asexual beings they are very inquisitive about this sin, known in the upper echelons as The Big One.

What will God's approach be? Is punishment the soup du jour? Or perhaps today is a chance for God to rain down mercy? That's what quite a few shaky-kneed souls at the front gates are hoping.

After the initial trumpet blast and fly past by the four horses of the Apocalypse, things quieten down considerably. A time for contemplation and furtive glances before a niggling sense of panic sets in. Does God know? Does he know the secrets of the human heart? What drives us to love and neglect and lie and pretend and caress and say goodbye? But more to the point, is it too late to repent or is the time now? No one wants to make the first move.

Bruce Baker (not his real name) from the Department of Philosophy at the University of Woolloomooloo looks uncomfortable. There is a persistent rumour circulating that the day will unfold in alphabetical order and 'B' is pretty up there. Surnames? Age? Occupation? No. It appears that God is working his way through on a national basis.

A wave of relief passes over Bruce as he realises how many countries are ahead of his: Albania, Algeria, Argentina...not to mention Antigua, Afghanistan...the Antipodes? That'll take at least the morning, thinks Bruce. He hops up onto one of the dazzling white communal hammocks that are free to use and with a swing to the right, a swing to the left, he's dead to the world.

Everything is not so hunky dory for Bruce's close companion, Kimberley (not her real name). With a surname like Aaronson (not her real surname), she is feeling tetchy. And her best friend, who happens to be Bruce's devoted wife of five years, is standing beside her. Smiling, what's worse. Bruce's wife is oblivious to the weekends her husband has spent in Kim's embrace. She thinks Bruce's lecturing take him to weekend camps for kiddies with learning difficulties, whereas Bruce's lechering takes him to weekend trysts with a cute netball player in a short pleated canary yellow skirt.

'Are you all right, Kimmie?' asks Bruce's devoted wife. 'You look pale.'

Kimberley smiles weakly and goes off to find a heavenly fountain spurting cool, clear water to wash her face, wash her hands, wash her sins away.

Afif (not his real name) is not feeling so bad as he waits for proceedings to commence. Indeed he is a little smug. With seven wives and twenty five children (two more on the way), he is hardly a candidate for 'Mr Adulterer of the Year'. But, still, there was that servant girl that could technically be classified as...

She wouldn't tell.

Afif frowns as it dawns on him that God knows. That's the whole point. Even if the servant girl has been shipped off to a seaside port across the gulf with a canvas bag, a blanket and some bread to eat, God knows. Afif squirms in his radiant white robes and flicks an imaginary blowfly over his shoulder for the third or fourth time. It's a nervous tic.

Suddenly, a brilliant revelation comes to him. He gives Bruce's wife, who happens to be looking his way, a glistening smile full of teeth and moustache. This is not *my* God, he thinks. I did not ask to be up here with all these apostates. Heaven is a huge meeting house full of concubines, with young virgins draped across polished wooden benches, their flawless pale skin exposed to the delight of the male eye. That is heaven, as it is written, and so enjoying the fruits of heaven on earth is nothing short of satisfying heaven's entry requirements.

Afif looks down from the clouds and for a moment he sees his favourite wife, bending over low, washing, her breasts dangling down like melons. He will miss her, but heaven awaits, and if it has in store what he thinks it does, he'll accept their permanent separation. But why does he suddenly feel this uneasiness, a pang of loneliness as if hope has gone? The blistering guilt of many years of failure as a husband and a father takes hold of him like icy fingers round his throat and he falls to his knees, a shivering wreck of seedy memories, plaintive cries for help that go unanswered and regrets.

Several huddled Azerbaijanis who are next in line glance over with admiration at this passionate man, believing him to have fallen on his knees in a revelry of joyous worship. Gail (her real name), a tall suntanned Californian, looks over and suspects the truth – that he is terrified of meeting his maker. She tosses her head defiantly. She has been to bed with so many married men over the last twelve years she has lost count but has not one iota of guilt because she sees herself as providing a service. She doesn't break up marriages, she enhances them. She certainly feels she has nothing to fear from this God character, even if she doesn't know whether she believes in Him.

'I mean, God takes history into account, doesn't he?' she waxes lyrical to her similarly tall, bronzed friend, Toby-the-personal-trainer (his real name), who looks for all the world like a braindead Adonis. 'God has to realise that people have changed. Humanity is different to a hundred years ago, a thousand years ago.'

Toby nods sagely.

'You can't let outdated moral codes dictate behaviour. Society is different. Relationships are different. Men expect different things from women today, for heaven's sake. There's, there's…'

'Steroids,' says Toby.

'Toby, I think you're in the wrong queue.'

And then there is Koji (his real name), the poorly paid swimming pool attendant, haunted for years by the beautiful Mrs A (not her real name), who frequented his swimming pool every Thursday morning. He fantasised about Mrs A but he could tell from her towel, her bathing costume and her strappy sandals that she was a woman with a capacity to spend money that he would never have. The beautiful Mrs A made him feel wretched yet glorious. How could he even stand in her presence? He contemplated stabbing himself to death with a snorkel and leaving a suicide note declaring his love for her, but he felt he would be letting the Council down. After all, he had worked there for nearly thirteen years. How would they possibly find a replacement?

One day his world changed when she spoke to him. In Japanese. 'The toilet in the women's change room is overflowing,' she said.

He went into fits of ecstasy and exited to fix it.

Why, he would plunge his bare arms up to his elbows in stinking effluent just to be near the beautiful Mrs A! He would bathe in the excrement of rabid raccoon dogs! He would shampoo his hair with the urine of a thousand green pheasants!

As he washed himself thoroughly, he heard her dainty pink footsteps behind him. She stood deliciously near and he could smell her perfume, a scent of vanilla, of rose petals, of everything fantastical and floral. In an instant she whisked out an exquisite tiny flask from her handbag and sprayed him with perfume, laughing.

'You smell beautiful!' she giggled in Japanese.

'You smell beautiful,' said Koji in Japanese, stumbling over the words, out of his mind by his proximity to the beautiful Mrs A. Mrs A in her voluptuously moulded swimming costume which miraculously never got wet.

And then it happened. Did she throw herself at him or did he plunge into her depths? Koji doesn't know. All he knows is that he made passionate love to her then and there in the women's change room and it was the most wonderful experience of his life.

He was dismissed from his job, not for having sex in the women's change room, but for performing a non-official duty. He should have left the toilet overflow to the plumber and not taken it upon himself to fix.

Even though he never saw the beautiful Mrs A again, he thought about her each day, every day, reliving those moments with her, deeply convinced that he loved her and that she loved him and that their love was the greatest love.

And now, waiting at the gates dreaming of Mrs A, Koji is the most serene of all. If what he has done is wrong, well, he will humbly accept his punishment, but he is so enraptured by what he thinks is love that nothing matters to him any more.

Nothing matters any more. Why is it so easy to get to that point? Deep deep down. Do we trust instincts, those poor squashed impulses that have been beaten and mauled by greed and hatred and too much noise? If love is blind, is passion blinder? Do we flaunt our private world and watch it explode on stage in a lurid exposé? Or do we live with restraint, never letting our secret desires loose from their cage?

Koji knows that the answers to these questions are not known. The time to answer them is not now. And the place where they are answered is the Other Place.

Black cats are traditional symbols of nastiness so I thought I would create a sinister white one. I had a blue-eyed white cat called Esky when I was growing up and, to me, Esky was the best cat ever. Our next door neighbours' cat was called Twistie which I thought was a wonderful name for a gingery kind of cat. Twistie had not a streak of malice in her, neither did Esky, unlike the cat in this story.

The White Cat

I'm in a helicopter, Sydney's northern beaches stretched out below. There's such a lot to see down there but I'm not really interested. I'm thinking about the white cat that killed my brother.

This joy ride is some kind of miserable compensation. The helicopter pilot is a friend of a friend who wanted to drag me out of my despair and offered me this free trip. I don't know why flying over the coast should make me feel better. There's white, white, white. The crests of chopping waves like crazed hairless guinea pigs rushing towards certain death. The clouds are white, the blinding sand is white, it's a symphony of white, no, a cacophony and I don't like it. It reminds me of the white cat.

I found my brother lying on the ground, bleeding badly. His hands were stretched out, his palms open in terror as if he was trying to tell me something or hoping that if he could just keep tensing those muscles, then his blood would keep pulsing and his heart would keep beating and he would go on living.

I'm looking down over dark squat hills that are too big to be hills, too small to be mountains. There's a misshapen lagoon, the hint of a muddy creek running below the canopy of trees, an ugly tangle of sunbaked roads shooting up the coast like the veins in my brother's arms, life pulsing through them, life running out.

Pussy cat, pussy cat, where have you been?

The white cat befriended my brother, not the other way round. She used to follow him up the three steps to my house and wrap around his ankles until he opened the front door. My brother would give her a piece of hamburger or sometimes milk just past its use-by date. Always something for that cat, a tasty treat for that ungrateful, disgusting animal. And how did it repay him? I suppose it's not unusual. Dogs have a loyalty beyond loyalty. They will guard their dead master, they will bear silent witness in times of hardship, strife and sadness. The dog mourns. The cat walks away.

We're buzzing familiar places from my childhood but they seem an infinity away. The landscape unfolds in neat predictable patterns. Gently rolling slopes of blue haze, little inlets and deep teal bays, very pretty. Why doesn't life unfold in the same way? When it does, it's boring, when it doesn't, it's hateful.

The bushland is magnificent, the silver grey shimmer vast and breathtaking. A place to be alone without being lonely. A refuge of serenity and purity. Except for the shrubs and weeds that take over and destroy it. What are those purple noxious ones that smother everything in sight? I think they are called Morning Glories.

Morning Glories. This morning will be a glorious morning.

My brother was up on a ladder, painting the inside of my new house. I'd gone to buy some milk, creamy, creamy milk for the wretched cat. My brother had just got out of gaol – six years for attempted armed robbery. We all have our failings and you don't have to believe me but he was the sweetest man you could ever meet. Everything was going right for him and I was so pleased. He was getting married in a month's time, he was genuinely happy. Painting the walls – a subtle mint berry if you're interested – was an enjoyable task and he was doing it so well. No dripping paint, no skimping with the undercoat, no missed corners on the cornices. My dear brother, the master craftsman.

He fell off the ladder while I was at the shops. The white cat knocked one of the legs of the ladder and made it fall, with a swish of its tail, with a sway of its rump. My brother broke his back from the fall so the autopsy said. He cut his arm on the metal tape measure or the paint tray or something, not bad enough to kill him, but he started to bleed.

I was standing outside the window, probably three metres from where my brother lay dying, chatting to the woman next door. I normally don't talk to neighbours but I liked this woman – she was friendly and down-to-earth – so we talked. All the time we were talking, my brother was dying and the white cat didn't make a sound. If it had, I would have gone inside and…

But the white cat didn't make a sound.

The autopsy said that my brother's eyes had been scratched out, possibly by a cat's claws. It must have been after he was dead or I would have heard him. The autopsy said he had scratch marks along his chest. Deep and festering. The kind made by a small animal, possibly a domestic cat. The autopsy said there were signs of suffocation – it is conceivable that his breathing passages were blocked by a considerable bulk about the size and weight of a domestic cat. The autopsy conjectured – although they are not supposed to do that, are they? – that my brother was smothered to death by a cat sitting on his face. And then the cat scratched his eyes out as a grand parting gesture of contempt.

The sound of a cat getting restless. A white cat, no less. How do I know? I have brought her with me on our little joy ride.

And now we begin our descent.

'Open the window,' I say.

The pilot laughs but it is not funny.

'Open the window,' I say again.

'The window?' the pilot says. 'Can't be done. We'll lose air pressure.'

'This isn't a plane. We're not flying high.'

He shakes his head.

I smash my hand through the front windscreen and he's right. The cabin starts to lose pressure.

'You maniac!' he yells, trying to keep control of the chopper.

I smile, the white cat struggling in my arms in an apparent attempt to participate in the excitement of the moment.

'You maniac!'

I hear the pilot again. Again. Caught on auto-pilot. Auto-pilot. You maniac. Maniac.

There isn't time to put on parachutes. There isn't time to radio for help. There isn't time. Above the deafening blur of wind and blades comes a sound that is music to my ears. A beautiful, beautiful noise.

Pussy cat, pussy cat is yowling in terror.

I throw the white cat out the window.

A crash, not half as frightening as I thought it would be. I feel pain in my arms and legs but nothing that can't be fixed with a little physiotherapy. There's a curdling animal cry, a whelp of exquisite pain which pleases me immensely. It's the white cat stumbling through the undergrowth towards me. But she doesn't come to me for she knows that if she did I would strangle her with my bloodstained hands. She slinks up to the pilot, who is still breathing, very, very faintly.

She draws her claws and sharpens them on his chest like he is a human whetstone. She drives them into his chest. I want to stop her but I can't. It appalls me, it fascinates me. He makes a strange gargling sound. I could go to him but I'm too fixed, too exhausted, too electric. She sits on his mouth and nose and looks across at me with a flick of her milky tail, triumphant.

See. I did this to your brother and now I will do it to your friend and then I will do it to you.

She raises her devil claws, ready to scratch his eyes out.

'No, pussy cat no!' I cry from across the grass. I crawl and I lunge and I grab its tail and raise it in the air and smash its head into the ground again and again and again. No pussy cat, no. I sigh a deep sigh of pain, more pain then I imagine could be possible. No, pussy cat, no.

I close my eyes and wait for retribution.

They will find my body beside a white cat and my hands will be stretched out, my palms open in terror like I was hoping that if I could just keep tensing those muscles, then my blood would keep pulsing and my heart would keep beating and I would go on living.

In my delirium I think I see the white cat slip away, leaving a creaming buttermilk trail of stars. But perhaps it was the spirit of the cat for I knew the cat was dead.

And now I am 80 years old, alone and lonely. Without children or grandchildren, nieces or nephews, without dog or goldfish or friend. I sit on the front porch of my little house every morning, watching the helicopters take off. And every evening I still see the white cat in my garden, a wicked fairy cat leaving a milky trail of starlight. My ghost cat will never leave me but she is so beautiful I don't mind her being here.

I originally called this *What if..?* but question marks in titles only complicate things. The inspiration came from researching the consequences of coming second, one example being Buzz Aldrin, the second man on the moon. Subsequently, I read a wacky book called *Buzz Aldrin, What Happened To You in All The Confusion?* by Johan Harstad because I loved the title and it was Nordic and vaguely relevant. To top it off, I discovered Dr Mae Jemison, the first African American woman in space, who said: **'Don't let anyone rob you of your imagination, your creativity, or your curiosity…'**[i]

But I Miss it

Who: Proserpine, first woman on the moon
                    Ceres, Personal Assistant to Proserpine
Where: A desolate planet that no one has ever
                    heard of
When: The future

PROSERPINE WHERE ARE YOU?

She takes deep gulps of air.

PROSERPINE I can hardly breathe.

Sees Ceres approaching.

PROSERPINE Why are you walking like that?
CERES   Lucky there's oxygen. Not much but —

PROSERPINE Oxygen? It's not as if we're in outer space. On a desolate planet that no one has ever heard of.

CERES There's no one. No one at all.

PROSERPINE But… My PA? My barista? That's not to say I need them.

CERES I'm your PA.

PROSERPINE Oh. What about my barista?

CERES You don't need them.

PROSERPINE Let's go.

CERES How many times — ? Our lunar module broke down.

PROSERPINE And no one is coming to help us —

CERES Remember?

PROSERPINE But I am the first woman to set foot on the moon. There's no one —?

CERES It's not that they don't want to help us. They can't. They can't get here. They don't know where here is. Do you know where here is? I DON'T KNOW WHERE HERE IS.

Pause.

PROSERPINE Look.

CERES The Earth.

PROSERPINE It's so – unearthly. Teensy weensy. What a funny shade of – what would you call that

CERES   Midnight blue.
PROSERPINE Deathly blue.

Admires her blue nail polish.

PROSERPINE Dark–defunct–dead–dagger–doomsday–
               blue. And the smell of ethyl acetate.

Breathes in blissfully then splutters.

PROSPERINE They love me down there. That's not
               the earth.
CERES   It is. It's just a long way away.
PROSERPINE My earth is filled with neutral buoy-
               ancy simulators, BA Hons in
               Communications fascinated with what I
               have to say, and guest spots on celebrity
               astronaut cooking shows. They love me
               down there. They love me. That can't
               be the earth.
CERES   It is. It's just more three dimensional
               than we give it credit for.
PROSPERINE My earth is full of fashion shoots with
               the latest in urethane coated–nylon, mi-
               crodermabrasion facials and my eighty
               four million, eight hundred and seventy
               four thousand, seven hundred and sev-
               enteen followers on twitter which puts

	me way–ahead–of–Taylor–Swift–just. They love me down there. They do. They love me.
CERES	So you keep telling me.
PROSERPINE	Or wherever the earth is – do I? – because I just can't believe that's the earth Let's go.
CERES	How many times —? There has been a breakdown in communication.
PROSERPINE	And no one is coming to help us —
CERES	Remember?
PROSERPINE	But I am the first woman to set foot on the moon. There's no one — ? I don't know what you mean. I like it here. It's calming. But I can see it getting on my nerves. And we do need to get to the Moon. So chop chop.

She looks around.

PROSERPINE What if — ? What if there were aliens?

She's delighted at what she sees.

PROSERPINELook! So many of them! Do you think they recognise me? What if I stand like — ?

Strikes a pose.

PROSERPINE They seem uninterested.
CERES Smile. Not too much —
PROSERPINE I've never met anyone not interested in me.
CERES — that's good.
PROSERPINE They know who I am, don't they?
CERES Keep walking.
PROSERPINE Like this?
CERES Look straight ahead and they won't eat you.
PROSPERINE Aren't they vegetarians?
CERES Watch out for that one. Careful. And that one. It's leering at you.
PROSERPINE [*to Ceres*] Why are you doing this? [*to alien*] Naughty boy. Girl. Thing.
CERES It can see into your soul.
PROSERPINE What if there's nothing there?
CERES Look at that one. NO! DON'T LOOK!
PROSERPINE What if —? What if they don't like me? What if they've beaten me to it? I must talk to them.
CERES Go ahead.
PROSERPINE [*to alien*] Our lunar module broke down. [*to another one*] Do you un–der–stand? [*to another*] And I am to be the first woman to set foot

	on the moon so we really have to get going. [*to another*] We are – [*to Ceres*] Are we slowly running out of oxygen? [*to alien*] We are slowly running out of oxygen.
CERES	[*joining in*] Are you familiar with orbital manoeuvring systems? [*to another*] Do you happen to have any monomethylhydrazine? [*to herself*] What am I doing?
PROSERPINE	Tell me again. Why are you walking like that?
CERES	We're in outer space. On a desolate planet that no one has ever heard of.
PROSERPINE	And no one is coming to help us. There's no one — ?
CERES	Being strong requires inhuman strength
PROSERPINE	I am the first, aren't I?
CERES	That's what this is all about.
PROSERPINE	When all the borders of all the countries in all the world were absolutely gobbled up and smothered with peace and prosperity and big ideas and the–sky's–the–limit and building what cannot be built and imagining what cannot be imagined someone somewhere came up with an astonishing possibility: What if — ? What if I was

<table>
<tr><td></td><td>the first woman to set foot on the
moon? I wanted it. I snatched it. I made
it happen. I snapped my fingers and —</td></tr>
<tr><td>CERES</td><td>Almost.</td></tr>
<tr><td>PROSERPINE</td><td>I gleam. I triumph.
I–am–what–do–you–mean–'almost'?</td></tr>
<tr><td>CERES</td><td>We're here. Not there. This is some-
where else. Do you know where here
is?</td></tr>
<tr><td>PROSERPINE</td><td>YOU DON'T KNOW WHERE HERE
IS. This is not the moon? Whose fault is
it? Is it yours?</td></tr>
<tr><td>CERES</td><td>Don't snap at me.</td></tr>
<tr><td>PROSERPINE</td><td>Did you do this to me? Why aren't I on
the moon? Where is the moon? Why
isn't this the moon? Is it sabotage? Ter-
rorism? It was that pointy faced
aeronautical engineer. She never liked
me. And that thrust chamber assembly
cluster —</td></tr>
<tr><td>CERES</td><td>I don't think so.</td></tr>
<tr><td>PROSERPINE</td><td>Let's go.</td></tr>
<tr><td>CERES</td><td>How many times —?</td></tr>
<tr><td>PROSERPINE</td><td>Three.</td></tr>
<tr><td>CERES</td><td>What?</td></tr>
<tr><td>PROSERPINE</td><td>Three. Three is a good number. Fi fie
fo. Tic tac toe. Piggy in the middle.
[*loudly & brightly, counting syllables*</td></tr>
</table>

	on her fingers] 'Do–you–know–the– [way to San Jose]? Bom–bom–bo–bo– bom–bom–bo–bom–bom…' Do you?
CERES	Yes.
PROSERPINE	They love me up here. They do. They love me. What if —? What if something happens? What if nothing happens? What if nothing happens ever again? This was going so well. I am the first. I can't stand this. I want air–conditioning. I am the first woman to set foot on the moon. I am. Yes, I am. I will be. I want to breathe. Not this. Don't want this. What do we do now? Endless days. Endless night. I want an appointment! I want an apartment! I WANT A MANICURE!

Ceres slaps her.

PROSERPINE	Remember Monica Le/winsky —
CERES	/No, no, no.
PROSERPINE	You must.
CERES	I don't want to.
PROSERPINE	Amy Winehouse? And Whitney Houston? Do you —?
CERES	Of course I remember —

PROSPERINE Peaches Geldof. And Antigone. And
Paula Yates. And Madame Bovary. And
Marilyn Monroe. And Marsh Mowbray. I remember when Mother Teresa
said — What did she say?

CERES 'There is such terrible darkness within
me – as if everything was dead.'[ii] Do
you know who said that?

PROSERPINE Is that a trick question?

CERES No.

PROSERPINE Who said that?

CERES I just told you.

PROSERPINE Who did? Some ungodly creature.

CERES MOTHER TERESA.

PROSERPINE Are you saying MOTHER TERESA is
UNGODLY?

Ceres shakes her head.

PROSPERINE Why did Marilyn Monroe die? Who is
Marsh Mowbray? Why are all these
women dead? What about me? That's
what this is all about. Forget about
them. It's me. I am the First Woman on
the moon. Has it taken place? Has it
happened? It has to be. It will be. Somewhere. Up here. Soon. Now.

Pause.

PROSERPINE I demand to be the First Woman on the
moon!

Pause.

PROSERPINE They love me down there. I am
more successful than you will ever
be. I am the first woman on the
moon – no wait, we're somewhere
else – it will be all right. When you
fix up the communications systems.
You should get onto that. Yes, that'
what you can do now. I command
you. While I will — I always felt
sorry for Marilyn Monroe. Frozen
in amber, alive, while at the same
time dead.

CERES The sad thing is she never knew.

PROSERPINE Knew what?

CERES That she achieved post–humous fame
on a ridiculous scale.

PROSERPINE Unless she's looking down on us.

CERES What absolute tosh.

PROSERPINE What if she is? She's looking down on
us. Just as we're looking down on
them. Imagine.

CERES　　　　　There is no one looking down on us. The dead have no interest in us. The living have no interest in us.

PROSERPINE　Does this mean I didn't make it?

CERES　　　　　You nearly made it.

PROSERPINE　That's not enough.

CERES　　　　　You need to fight.

PROSERPINE　What if I'm too tired?

CERES　　　　　Get a sub–machine gun. Mow down twenty school children and the principal and four teachers and —

PROSERPINE　Stop it.

CERES　　　　　You must do something. You haven't blown up an entire city with an atomic bomb, have you? Or shot seventy seven students dead on an island off the coast of Norway?

PROSERPINE　No.

CERES　　　　　You haven't let a million of your own people starve to death in the name of agrarian utopia. You didn't blast two hundred and ninety eight people out of the sky over Ukraine. That's how it is on this something or other of an earth.

PROSERPINE　A godforsaken place.

CERES　　　　　What if darkness is falling for the first time? And our true natures are about to be revealed? What if we

keep our eyes transfixed on the
Earth? And tell stories.

PROSERPINE I don't like stories.
CERES You do.
PROSERPINE I don't know any.
CERES You know thousands.
PROSPERINE I never tell them right.
CERES THAT'S BECAUSE YOU NEVER
LISTEN.

Proserpine slaps her.

CERES If only you appreciated what you had.

They gaze at the Earth.

CERES I was there when Joan of Arc lay siege
to Orléans. With the sword of Saint
Catherine de Fierbois held high, surging
into battle on her foaming white horse.
PROSERPINE It was chestnut. And she got burned at
the stake. And you weren't there.
CERES I was. She won the Star of Gallantry for
valour and had her portrait painted by
Artemisia Gentileschi and opened a
high class brothel and retired to a Cas-
tle on a Cloud with Alice in
Wonderland. And Boadicea —

PROSERPINE Don't tell me you were there too.
CERES She gave the Romans what for. I saw her. Eyes blazing, braver than a hundred hungry lions, triumphant in her chariot of gold.
PROSERPINE And then she killed herself.
CERES What if she didn't? What if she went on to have her own management consultancy and dedicated her life to raising money to save the Cottontop tamarin by swimming the English Channel nineteen times non–stop without any clothes on every year on the first of March until she turned seventy seven?
PROSERPINE That would be Spring. In the northern hemisphere. What did she do? When she turned seventy seven?
CERES She became a lion tamer.
PROSERPINE That's a good story.
CERES I was there when Marie Curie won the Nobel Prize. Twice.
PROSERPINE No.
CERES She did. Once for physics. Once for chemistry. The only person who has ever won the Nobel Prize in two different sciences.
PROSERPINE What if she won it more than that? Three times, four, six hundred and

sixty six times? Not just for science but for literature and fire–eating and being woodchopping champion at th Easter Show and for inventing de-signer handbags with magic interiors that have no bottom or sides? Wher else have you been?

CERES I flew across the Atlantic with Amelia Earhart.

PROSERPINE So did I! Wasn't that fun? What if she had flown so high that she hit her head on the Sun? And she ended up here? And any second now she'll come rounc the corner – not that there is a corner – and say hello? In a southern kind of ac cent like Dorothy. She was from Kansa too, you know. Do you have a camera? Do you think she'll recognise me? Won't it be wondrous?

CERES It will be an extraordinary moment.

PROSERPINE Just like the time I — I remember walk ing to the podium. The applause and the clamouring and the attention of the world on me.

CERES I remember walking over sand. Tiny fish darting in the rock pools. And the sandstone swirling like caramel ice cream.

PROSERPINE I am to be the first woman to set foot
on the moon. The glare and the glam-
our and the almighty expectations of
the world on me, spiralling around me,
all leading to —
CERESE And the cormorants dive–bombing and
then spreading their wings like angels
of death. And the sand crunching. And
the smell of sunlight.
PROSERPINE Sunlight doesn't —
CERES Yes it does. Better than ethyl acetate.
Ten thousand times better than oxy-
gen. The best smell in the world.
And my little girl's hair, full of sand,
flopping over her eyes, wet with
sand, always sand.
PROSERPINE I didn't know you — I didn't know you
liked the beach.
CERES You never asked. He did.
PROSERPINE Who?
CERES Hamlet.
PROSERPINE Hamlet?
CERES Asked. All those questions. Didn't have
a clue. But Ophelia. She knew.
PROSERPINE Does this mean I didn't make it?
CERES You nearly made it.
PROSERPINE That's not enough. I need to…[fight].
Will I ever see…[my family again]?

What if…[I don't make it]? Tell me what Ophelia knew.

CERES Sometimes it is easier not to be.

PROSERPINE That's not a nice thing. But you can think it, can't you? Even if it's not nice, do you think —?

CERES I think we should be full of imagination. I think the Earth is unjust and fantastical and maddening. But I miss it.

PROSERPINE I miss it too. Good night.

Proserpine lies down.

CERES Good night.
PROSERPINE Sweet dreams.
CERES Sweet dreams.
PROSPERINE See you in the morning.

Ceres folds her space jacket lovingly, places it on ground, and lies down next to Proserpine.

I love the mass-produced, packaged world of 1960's pop: The Turtles, The Easybeats, The Loved Ones, The Zombies, The Foundations, Paul Revere and the Raiders, it goes on and on... Not to mention all those fabulous Girl Groups and soloists like The Shirelles, The Shangri-Las, Bev Harrell, Lynne Randell, Cilla, Petula and Dusty. She had the sultriest voice. Not hot and sexy like Etta James. Not crystal clear like Judith Durham. Smooth and rich and effortless. A truly 'dusty' kind of voice.

Dusty Springfield's Voice

No one expected anything to happen that Sunday afternoon in the cemetery. It was a gentle summer's day. A handful of walkers meandered through the overgrown grass, gazing up at the chalky marble angels silhouetted against the sky. There was a young woman, forlorn at the grave of her lost boyfriend recently drowned. Hardly a sound. The breeze between the trees. A crow's agonised cry. A bubbling thick silence descended on the rows of gravestones.

Beneath the surface, there was a presence. It strained and strained for it was only small. It rose up from the grave, pushing up the damp earth in its quest for freedom. It struggled to the surface, nudging its way until it almost broke through the hardened dirt. For even if she was dead, it was not ready to die.

It was fluid, velvet, the colour of warm lavender. It was indescribable but perfectly describable. A voice. The voice that melted people's hearts, the voice that could be mournful or joyful, exuberant or mellow. It was a voice that required nothing. No one could train it, no one could coax it. She – when she was alive – never made an effort to sing. It simply came out of her, the way some people cannot stop talking. She could not stop singing. And when she died, the voice lay dormant for a while, wondering what to do. And then it decided to rise again.

What was it? It was stronger than steel and lighter than air. It had no feet and no hands but it could fly and dart and persevere. It could sing but it couldn't talk. It knew what it couldn't possibly know and acted on impulse. It was intelligent. It was life. Where would it go? It didn't concern itself with practicalities. It was out. It would find a way.

It was the voice of Dusty Springfield.

On gossamer wings it flew to a beautiful old church where it danced with specks of dust floating in the rays of light streaming in through the stained glass. That night when the young pastor sang *Kyrie Eleison*, the voice that came out was not his own. He blushed as a sweet gentle voice filled the church. The congregation's collective eyes widened but they said nothing. He blushed again. The voice knew that what it had done was not right. It knew that the body it had inhabited didn't feel right. This new body was not glad or comfortable. It was stricken with embarrassment. And so the voice fled into the night. Invisible yet distinctly visible, a shadow, a breath.

It fled to a drunken brawling pub where a woman swayed while her sweaty hands clung to a microphone. The voice came out of her and her rendition of *My Way*. The audience gasped. No one knew she could sing like that. The barman was in tears. The woman's husband was in tears. But the voice didn't like the woman. Her body was dank and creaking and she didn't seem grateful or pleased. She kept drinking and decided she wanted to sing another song. She grabbed the microphone greedily. Her husband tried to stop her. The voice escaped.

The wind began to shriek and the voice looked up to it with a question. It picked up the voice and swept it along a wide road into a huge gleaming building with stark corridors that led to a small white room. A girl lay in a starched deathly bed, her mother leaning over her with fear in her eyes.

'Let's sing the song we used to sing when you were a little girl,' said the mother. The girl shook her head. She didn't want cheering up. She wanted to die.

'Let's sing the song…'

The mother swallowed and open her lips but the nurse came in and took her outside. The mother looked back, knowing that the girl's gesture of defiance was final.

The voice hovered in the room for it had nowhere else to go. It felt death breathing. The little girl had no desire, the drunken woman had no respect, the young pastor had no confidence.

'Who wants me?' asked the voice. 'Who wants this voice?'

But the air-conditioning was too loud, the lifts too busy, the corridors filled with shuffling white-coated people trying to find beds.

'Who will have this voice?'

And then it heard a wondrous sound. Amidst the sterile clatter, a sound called her. A lapping of waves, a swirl of water. The voice floated about the streets until she came to the water at the end of the world. As the lights came up and the sky darkened for another black night, the voice breathed in the salt.

This is beautiful, she thought. I have found something. Something that cannot be valued. Something that cannot cause shame, cannot cause pain.

She watched the patterns of light on the water. She watched the reflections of the buildings at the water's edge stretch and contort. She watched the choppy silver waves grow wilder and wilder.

The voice was happy. She screamed out to the darkness and flung herself into the ocean where an old fishing boat lurching with a full load of fish crushed her to death. No one saw. No one heard.

David McComb, lead singer of The Triffids, was an exceptional lyricist and songwriter. His words and music captured the essence of Australia, its rawness, vastness and heat along with its agony and desolation. I remember seeing Jill Birt and Alsy MacDonald get on a bus along New South Head Road near Rose Bay one Saturday night a long time ago. They were going to a party and asked if it was the right bus. I was young and amazed that such superstars were catching the bus.

Vale David McComb

(17 February 1962 – 2 February 1999)

* * *

She don't belong here anymore
Learn it the hard way it wasn't
Meant to be you it was meant for
Someone else but God has other plans you know
His whims it's
Everywhere in your lyrics Saint
Christopher and sacred hymns and landscapes
Like those walked it's in your rhythm
Your breath your lines your lows
Your highs I bet there weren't many
Of them Dear Jesus he is dead and
All the things he sang about you could
You could at least remember him in some
Way maybe a tree or a stretch of
Sand or a shed

* * *

* * *

You were the chamber of choristers
The mad poet
The knight on a wild white stallion
The descent the abyss
You calmed you taunted
You never forgave
Like Dylan Thomas
Rage rage against the dying of the
Old church in Paris covered in
You were the cynic
The seer
You could have been my brother
From far away
From a long long time before
When the world had joy
And you were innocent

* * *

* * *

Red ponies dance across the fields
Their hoofs in time with time itself
A red mane streaming in the wind
Red nostrils flaring
Red flanks and red thighs
But what colour are your eyes?
Beautiful one
You will run across the fields now
You will hear the canter of horses that don't exist
You will pluck grape vines weighed down
    with invisible fruit
A red pony will nuzzle your hand
And you'll be home

* * *

Both my parents are spending their final days with dementia. The best word I can think of to describe dementia is 'cruel'. It robs people of dignity, it sucks out their souls and it is undefeatable. Those left to care for those with dementia enter a period of mourning even though the people they love are not yet dead. It can last for years. A poem for my mother, my father and my brother.

Three Poems

* * *

Swallow

She lies in a state of half-living
The side of her face yellowed with bruises
She smiles She strokes my hair She looks scared
And in pain

I make a cup of tea. I mention them and she
    points to their photo on the wall

She can hardly form words She can hardly
    Swallow She can hardly be said to be
        Enjoying any kind of fucking quality of
            Life Sadness invades the very biscuit
                She tries to eat You have gone
                    Forever dearest soul

* * *

* * *

Two Years From Then

He is sprawled on the floor
Sleeping fitfully like a wounded animal
Coiled body, legs flung out
>Like a maddened King Lear who wanders
>alone in a state of desolation searching for
>who knows what & trying to get to who
>knows where and God only knows who would
>smile upon him now. My dear upright
>dignified father now you are a shape, a
>form, a mindless repetition of movement and
>sleep and nothing else no nothing else

* * *

* * *

Mooney Mooney

Clay ash like waste dumped in a toxic river
Then the water washes the leaden mass away
Specks fall, fragmented tiny magical
The tide carries the last small dot of life away
And Warwick is gone

* * *

Statues are a link between the living and the dead. My first play *Statues of David* was inspired by the true story of a 47-year-old unemployed Italian who smuggled a hammer into the Galleria Dell'Accademia in Florence and smashed David's left foot, breaking the second toe. Police described him as 'deranged' but I like to think there was more to it. This little piece shines a new light on another iconic marble statue.

Do Not Touch

Who: Senior Constable Delores
Where: Local Police Station
When: Saturday Night

She was in quite a state. Half naked. Confused. Cold as marble. I put a blanket around her but it kept slipping off like melting ice.

I kept staring at her arms. I couldn't help it. Who did this to you? Who did this?

She had a wild look in her eyes. Like she was staring right through me to a thousand years ago. Two thousand. Maybe more.

Do you want a cup of tea? Do you know where you are? Do you understand? I wanted to grab her and shake her but –

I shut up. For maybe thirty seconds. Only then did she turn to me. Not from around here. No family here. She said – her true home was an island. Milos. Mellow? Milo? Can't read my writing.

She remembered a room. Large and airy. Lights on twenty four seven. Go on, I said. Not just her, there were others. All in the same room. Kept, she said, more or less on display. Locked in at night. In the next breath she claimed they treated her well.

Classic Stockholm syndrome.

What happened in the room? Nothing. I tried again. Can you tell me anything? Anything at all? People came and looked at her. Men? No, she said. Yes, she said. Men. Women. Children. Did they pay you? [*shakes head*] They paid to come in but she never saw any money. Get this: no one was allowed to touch her. There were signs: DO NOT TOUCH.

I left the room. What kind of place??? And then I came back.

[*gently*] What did you do while they watched? She insisted she didn't do anything. They just looked at her.

Pole dance? She frowned. Did you pole dance? I'm not here to judge. I want to help. You've lost your top, you show signs of –. Have you been – violated – in some way? She gazed through me. Blank. Are you a – sex worker? A whore?

She stood there, deathly white, her mouth ever-so-slightly twisted.

I am not a cheap scarlet-lipped harlot.

You're telling me you've been kept in a locked room? You're telling me people pay good money to look at you standing there like a statue?

I am a statue.

What?

I was presented to the King himself, Louis the eighteenth.

Louis the – ? How old are you? [*flicks through notes*] Listen love, it's a legal requirement if you need a bit of help with Centrelink or anything like that. She took a deep breath and said she was two thousand one hundred and thirty years old.

Oh yes, I said. That's how we're going to play it? What's your name? Venus. [*jots it down*] Venus de Milo. What's the D for? Nothing. Venus. Venus. Where have I heard that before? You play tennis?

Told me she'd been in Paris for the last hundred years where she was much admired. In the Loo or something.

I am regarded as a work of art combining elements of the Hellenistic and Classical periods. A great beauty. Of historical significance.

[*splutters*] You got to laugh.

You are a barbarian.

What?

A barbarian.

I was born here, petal, not like some people. I don't know who brought you up but we have respect and tolerance in this society. So you can just zip your lip.

That look. That look was getting to me. Cold, hard bint.

I hate to point out – Ms D. Milo – but you have no arms. Not a good look. How did it happen anyway? Who did it to you? You can't remember, eh? Or you won't remember. Were you asking for it? See what I'm getting at? You're in denial. You're blocking out the past.

I had her.

This arm thing. Get a grip. You're not in good shape. You're old. You're chipped. You're not exactly a paragon of feminine gorgeousness. Who'd give you a second glance? I mean at least the Mona Lisa's got a bit of personality.

Why don't you go back to Milo or Marshmallow or wherever it is you come from and figure out how to make yourself useful. Some of us like to contribute to society, you know. We have jobs. We work for a living. But you. Historical significance? Get away. Beautiful? Broken, more like it. Take a good look at yourself. We don't need any more works of art around here, thank you very much *[slams folder shut]*.

She stared at me. Right into me this time. You're right, she said. I have no story. I have no past. I have nothing to give. And a shadow moved across her face – I swear I saw it – and she shut down. Wouldn't move. Couldn't move. Move along, I said. Move along. She couldn't hear. There were people waiting. Gets busy at this time on a Saturday night. Move along. Fixed. Resolute. Mute. Never seen anything like it. She couldn't move – [*falls silent, opens folder, looks through notes, closes folder*].

A barbarian.

Years ago I saw a random book on a shelf at Five Dock library with the word BLOCK in BLOCK capitals. I picked it up and found it was written by Lawrence BLOCK. On the basis of this word – BLOCK, no less – I borrowed it and discovered a breathtakingly prolific crime writer. I admire his – indeed any writer's – ability to plot a suspense story with only two characters and still keep you guessing.

SPOTTED

Miranda and Tom are heading back from an afternoon at Palm beach. Waves could have been higher for Tom and less sandy for Miranda, but as far as lazy summer days go, it was adequate. Tom is driving as usual, not that Miranda doesn't want to drive, but Tom assumes it is his role to take the wheel. Still, she drives a lot in her job so she doesn't mind.

The late afternoon sun hits the front windscreen and reflects Miranda's spotted skirt in the passenger window. Miranda stares at the reflection. Exquisite scarlet and cream fabric with handsewn beading by talented seamstresses (or perhaps peasants) of unknown nationality that must have taken weeks. Boy, did she pay for it. Pity it will be out of fashion by the end of January. Still, a season's wear is a season's wear and this skirt has seen the inside of countless board rooms, hotels and planes. And, of course, the inside of Carlo's car.

Tom never comments about Miranda's clothes but Carlo always notices. He calls it her señorita skirt – even though he is Italian – thanks to the flounce along the bottom cut across the bias. The colour suits you, he says, it is a scarlet rose for my rose. Silently repeating the words to herself as Tom drives home, they have a ridiculous ring to them, but at the time, as she lay in his arms under a hazy sky, they were the most romantic thing anyone had ever said. Like being told your skin is marble or your locks raven black.

She looked at the skirt in the mirror and saw another reflection – the silver ring on her middle finger. A gift from her mother. The first time she wore it, her friends made complimentary remarks about Tom's taste in jewellery. She let them think he had bought it because it was easier that way. The ring shone against the rosy glow of her scarlet skirt and she almost smiled. But she'd spent the afternoon picking away at an old argument with Tom, a scab that kept oozing, and she didn't want him to think things were all right. They were not all right.

Carlo's car.

Carlo's car was approaching in her side mirror. Unmistakable, since there were only twelve of them in the entire country or so he said. She was amused by Carlo's continual attempts to impress her with his toys: his car (admittedly sublime), his mobile (so-so), his cufflinks (tiny compasses, of all things…), his robotic vacuum cleaner (dubious, to say the least), his $28,000 mag sports shoes (he was, she had to accept, a fan of *Back to the Future*).

It was a mutually acknowledged game they played. Carlo pretended to be offhand about his latest acquisition and she pretended to be enamoured. Behind his feigned indifference he was as excited as a four-year-old boy given a bunny rabbit and she – grounded firmly in reality – couldn't care less. She often wondered why she was so attracted to Carlo. He was the antithesis of everything that was decent. All he cared about was the shadow of things. Marty McFly was his favourite screen character of all time, for goodness' sake. But he was energetic, he had goals. He was certain and strong and full of conviction. He was on his way somewhere. She could not help but adore him.

Love him? No. But he was grounded in the city and so was she. The city bars, city fashion, city gyms and meeting places. She loved being swept up in all that. Tom had grown up in a small town and he was keen to return. He hinted at moving but she never took the hint. He told her that he had changed but she didn't see the change. He told her that she had changed. She disagreed. Violently. She lived for the city and the thought of some ugly backwater made her feel dead inside.

The side mirror had remarkable clarity.

Carlo's car shot past, 50 kilometres above the speed limit at the very least. A flash of impressions of the car she was so familiar with – Carlo's dark unruly hair, the silver grey upholstery of the empty passenger seat and a dark green bundle in the back seat – a picnic rug perhaps? Strange since Carlo detested outdoor dining unless it was under a large umbrella in a café that sold poké bowls.

She could not hide the thrill as he tore past. She crossed and uncrossed her legs, focusing on the beads of her scarlet spotted skirt. She imagined Carlo and her stretched out on Lido, waiter approaching with a silver tray bearing two milky cocktails. Carlo would reproach the waiter for spilling a minute drop of liquid on the tray. He wasn't afraid to demand the best. Unlike Tom who plodded along, not a man of great inspiration. Would Tom ever suggest going away for a weekend together? No. If she suggested it, he'd be pleased to go. But the idea would never cross his mind. The beach this afternoon was her idea.

'Better get some petrol.'

Predictable old Tom.

* * *

Tom pulled in alongside Carlo's car and Miranda felt that thrill again. The most exquisite sensation. Here was her husband parked alongside her lover, one knowing of the existence of the other, but with no idea of what he looked like. The other knowing nothing. The driver's seat was empty. Carlo must be paying for his petrol.

'Look,' Tom said, pointing, 'haven't you been looking for coriander?'

That was true. She had been wanting to make Thai coconut and coriander chicken. How interesting of him to remember.

As Tom filled the tank, she crossed the road to the garden shop but thoughts of Carlo crushed her thoughts of herbal delights. Where could he be tearing off to on a Sunday afternoon? She knew he had a sister – a timid little thing from his accounts – perhaps she lived somewhere up this way. Of course, he could be in pursuit of another business deal. Whoever invented the notion of Sunday as a day of rest didn't know Carlo. How many nights had he cancelled dinner with her, or just a drink, because he couldn't pull himself away from a clincher. She smiled ruefully. It always annoyed her but, conversely, she luxuriated in the times they did spend together when he transferred that intense focus to her, and only her.

At least he had something that drove him. That's what he was: a driven man. And she adored him and admired it at the same time as she was a little scared. She had never been driven in her life except in the passenger seat. What was it that caused people to find such pleasure in their work? Such meaning? Maybe he did it for the money – just like her – only there was more money at stake for him. Take his car.

Her eyes swept over the shiny silver body, the sexy Italian sunroof, the smooth low-slung curve of the rear. And that green picnic blanket.

* * *

Tom started the engine.

'Where's the coriander?'

'What? Oh...'

She told him that the only coriander they had was wilting and then absently asked if there was anyone else in the shop.

'In the shop?'

'Was anyone paying for petrol?'

'No.'

His tone of voice indicated that he thought it was a stupid question. She looked back as they were about to pull out from the service station.

'Wait. I need to go to the toilet.'

He slowed to a halt. Other men would have said: 'Well, why didn't you go when I was getting the petrol?'

She went into the shop. No sign of Carlo.

'Toilets?'

'Round the side,' the thin middle-aged assistant nodded. He was Indian or Pakistani, she thought, and neatly dressed. If everyone took such pride…

She went round the back and found the Ladies and the Gents and a smell entwining them that was not compelling.

'Carlo?' she breathed gently.

She poked her head in the Gents. No sign of Carlo. Where was he? Could he be in the Ladies? No. She poked her head in there anyway.

She returned to the shop.

'Excuse me. Excuse me!' she shouted until the assistant emerged from the room at the back.

'Has a man with dark wavy hair come in here?'

He looked at her blankly.

'The man who owns that car.'

She pointed at Carlo's car.

'A lady drives that car.'

'A lady?'

He nodded.

'Where did she go?'

'Across road to buy some herbs.'

'But that was me! I'm looking for a man. That car belongs to a man.'

'This man there?'

He pointed out the window at Tom.

'No, no, that's my husband. Thank you.'

She stepped outside, uneasy. A lady driver? Where was Carlo? It's possible he had taken an important phone call and was somewhere close by…

'Darling,' Tom said, leaning out the window, 'what are you doing?'

'Nothing.'

She sneaked another admiring glance at Carlo's car. How did he keep it so shiny? How did he have the time? That green picnic blanket. A niggling doubt took hold of her. It seemed incongruous given his capacity for non-stop work. He had never taken her on a picnic. Or even suggested it. Perhaps he was going on a picnic with someone else. A romantic, sensual, hazy picnic…

She gasped.

The green picnic rug on the back seat moved. She stared hard, hoping that somehow she would see through the glass more easily if she tried harder. She could swear it had moved. There was something underneath. Or someone.

'Darling?' Tom again.

She coughed.

'Sorry, I was feeling faint.'

'We have to get moving.'

'Yes, yes.'

How could she explain to her husband that something was wrong? How could she explain that she knew the owner of the silver car and he wasn't any-where and she was worried?

She got back into the car.

'There's something wrong.'

He looked at her thoughtfully.

'There's something in the back of that car,' she said. 'There's something on the seat. Under the blanket. It moved.'

'Miranda…'

'It moved.'

'Maybe it's a cat. Someone's taking a cat to the vet. What does it matter?'

'He doesn't like —'

'Who doesn't like —?'

'No one.'

Tom revved the engine.

'Let's go,' he said.

She is hysterical now.

'It's moving! There's something moving!'

She screams at him, clawing at the door to get out.

'All right,' he says with quiet fury, banging his hands on the steering wheel. 'Let's get to the bottom of this.'

He gets out of the driver's seat, goes round to her side and yanks her out of the car. He pulls her over to the silver car and forces her face up against the window. All she can think of is that Carlo will be furious because her cheek is leaving oily streaks on his polished glass.

'There is nothing moving. Do you see? There is nothing in the car,' he whispers viciously.

She tries to nod but can't. He has her by the scruff of the neck, keeping her face pressed against the window.

'Do you see? There is nothing.'

'Yes, yes,' she pleads. 'Please let me go.'

He releases her and she sees him in a different light.

'Now,' he says, 'let's find the mystery man. Let's find whoever drives this car since you seem to be so obsessed with him.'

'No, no,' she says. 'There's no need —'

'You said you tried the toilets.'

'Did I —?'

'Let's try them again.'

He looks grim.

'This is silly, Tom —'

He pulls open the door of the Ladies and shoves her inside.

* * *

Tom emerges a short time later flicking water from his hands. Back in the shop he palms a bundle of hundred dollar notes to the man behind the counter.

'Who was driving the silver car?' he asks.

'A lady,' says the service station attendant.

Tom gives a small nod and leaves.

A yellow mini Cooper pulls up and a young woman jumps out. She dashes round the corner to the toilet and emerges immediately, white-faced and mute. In a haze of horror she makes her way to the service station attendant and tells him what she has seen. A beautiful woman, a scarlet spotted skirt wrapped around her neck, like a poisonous snake strangling the life out of someone.

Someone who was on her way somewhere.

Tom flings his car keys into the bushes and walks towards the silver car where Carlo is sitting smoking a cigarette, sunroof up, a look of languid amusement on his face. Tom gets into the passenger seat and slides his hand along Carlo's inner thigh. Carlo blinks and starts the car. As the engine roars into action there is a small shriek.

Trust – that was hiding under the picnic blanket – lies still.

Dead.

A brutal homicide took place one winter's day in Sydney in 2001. A 20-year-old methodically murdered his sister, his mother and his father over a three hour period and then spray painted 'Fuck off Asians' on the living room wall so that police would think it was a racially-motivated hate crime. It was a hate crime but it was the hatred of a son towards his own flesh and blood.

One Syllable Beginning with 'S'

I am stripped of my external belongings but they cannot touch the jubilation bubbling inside me.

I am not an Alpha male. Some would say I am short and not particularly muscular but I have other weapons. My raw intelligence. My angelic face. My heavenly singing voice. I am uncertain of what use they can be put to in the correctional centre environment but that does not perturb me. I have body building magazines. My body and my bed. I can zone in to this artificial world and feel it is truly my home.

They say there will be no parole but I don't believe them. I will charm them as I have done before. I will flutter my eyelashes.

Do I miss my family? Ache for their presence? Their touch?

I miss my car.

* * *

My parents are virtuous God-fearing people. They have given me life, guidance and protection. My father is a giant of a man, a role model I could never aspire to because, well, I am not he. He is the immigrant, forever grateful to his adopted country for the chance to succeed, eternally beholden to his incomprehensible God for his family and his life. But his gratitude turns to obsequiousness as he strives so hard to succeed that he loses sight of what success is and why he should be devoting himself to such a thing. I think he truly believes that building wealth to create a stable, loving home is the ultimate success. Perhaps he is right. I prefer to think of success as getting what you want, preferably without the need to work at all. Work smarter, not harder, someone said. I don't know who. The whole charade of getting up every morning and going to work and coming home is curiously antiquated to me. I like the idea that you put on your Calvin Klein business shirt and your Zegna suit and look the part. My father is always well-dressed, the successful business man. I wouldn't say under any circumstances that he is a snappy dresser. Just well-dressed. There is a difference.

My mother, the dutiful ever-loving wife, is equally as ambitious as my father but she does not show it. Always by his side. Holding his hand. Behind him.

I do not mock her subservience. It is absolutely admirable and shows great strength of character. She is a conservative repressed dull dull dull old biddy – nearly fifty years old, for goodness' sake – who may once have been enticing but is now worn down from being an overly devoted employee, wife, mother and all-round put upon relative. She does everything right so why does her whole life seem wrong?

Oh, I almost forgot. There's me.

And my sister. Yes, I have a sister. How she looks up to me, her older-by-two-years brother. She is blossoming with the suggestiveness of supple sensuality. She will turn 18 tomorrow.

* * *

Family conversation at present revolves around my study habits.

'You must study. Harder. You must put your head down.'

'I do.'

'Last year, you did not do so well. This year, you must do better. Improve.'

'I will.'

'Improve. Improve your mind and your attitude.'

'Yes, Mumma.'

They discuss me behind my back. My father tells my mother to say these things to me because that is what he believes is the mother's role. And she does so but she is only doing what she is programmed to do.

Aren't we all?

She puts her pedicured foot down.

'You cannot have the car tonight. You cannot go out tonight.'

'That's not fair.'

'It is fair. You have not done what is expected of you.'

'I tried.'

'You did not. Give me the car keys.'

I don't listen to her. Well, only when she mentions 'car'. She is referring to my lime green Citroën, a gift from my beloved Mumma and Pappa on the illustrious occasion of my eighteenth birthday. The light of my life. The beauteous centre of my being. The glorious shape and form that makes me realise the extent of my desire. The day Pappa handed the car keys to me, I became aware of just how delicious the material world is. My car. My space. My universe. I am noticed. People watch as I drive by. They look at me. I like the magnetism of the metal. When I come into a large sum of money in the not-too-distant future I shall buy another car. And another. I think I will stop at five cars. I can park two in the garage, one at the side of the house, one in the carport and one will have to be parked on the street which is less than ideal but I can put up with it for a time.

I will sell my parents' cars.

My mother (with my father's full endorsement) threatens to limit usage of my car or even take it away. I look at her placidly but I am enraged.

'Mumma, I need the car. I need it to get to the university.'

'You can catch the bus.'

'I can't catch the bus.'

I realise with disgust that my voice is quivering.

'Other students catch the bus. There is a bus stop outside.'

'I don't like that idea.'

How dare she make such a threat. Once given, a gift such as this cannot be taken away. At least not from me. Does she not know how much my world revolves around that piece of achingly sexy machinery? My parents have no concept of how much of life is artifice. They see only concrete things like timetables and cheque books and the Royal College of Physicians.

You see, their wish for me is to become a surgeon. A brain surgeon. Or a heart surgeon. What does it matter? I would enjoy making incisions but not the preparation and concentration required. And I would get bored easily. 'Not another bloody aorta,' I would joke to the diminutive blonde in the tight skirt on my left who would bend close to wipe the sweat from my learned brow. And I would smell her and go crazy with desire but maintain all composure. Not because I am professional. Not because I respect her. But because I don't want another black mark against my name.

My HSC results were such a black mark. A massive nuclear bomb blast-sized black blot against my name. To my esteemed parents, not to me. To put it succinctly, my marks were not up to scratch.

My father wailed, 'My son, my son, how can you do this to me?'

'I haven't done anything to you.'

'We want you to do well. All we want is for you to succeed. We give you good schooling, tutors, support, encouragement. This is how you repay us?'

I bowed my head. I learnt long ago that attempting to discuss my academic performance with my father was not a good use of my time.

* * *

I enrol in a Science degree because they have the ridiculous notion that I will switch to Medicine next year. My results thus far have not been outstanding but they are unaware of this as I have creative ways of suppressing negative news re: my progress. Forged transcriptions. Stolen medical certificates to avoid exams. That sort of thing. The fact is I am bored witless at university. My intellectual ability is peerless as my parents recognise. But it cannot be confined to anti-quated institutions that require rigour, commitment and any kind of effort. Sitting in lecture theatres, clip-boards and note-taking? Only mindless morons fill their days with such as this. I would rather daydream of wealth while driving in my lime green Citroën.

I am raw intelligence and exquisite beauty.

I am beyond listening and learning.

On the other hand, my parents are creatures of habit. Unutterably pedestrian. I know their every movement. How I detest them.

My mother will arrive home from work at 4.30pm. My father will walk in the door at six o'clock on the dot.

And my sister. She will be upstairs in her bedroom, studying virtuously. Did I tell you she turns 18 tomor-row?

I have two kitchen knives and a baseball bat.

* * *

I pull up in the carport and sit in my car for a moment or two.

The three yapping Malteses. I will lure them into the laundry with warm milk and paint stripper.

The side door I will leave open so that when our neighbour drops by, she will knock and get no answer. She will knock again and think: how strange.

She will go around the side of the house, see the open door and…

I will think of nothing else until it is done.

* * *

Afterwards.

I go out for dinner with my friend. Why not? I am a master of indifference. And it's his shout. I pick him up at eight o'clock and we drive into town. On the way, I mention my afternoon's activities in case he needs them for a police interview in the future. I tell him I drove out to Bankstown, looking for a friend's house, but I couldn't find it. That's how I spent the last four hours.

Planet Hollywood. I have lost my appetite. I don't understand why.

'Food poisoning,' I say. That's always a good one.

I talk up my conquests. There is a girl the year ahead of me. I am desperate for her. Groaning.

'Man, oh, man,' I tell my friend, 'She is so hot.'

'How far have you got?'

I give him a look.

I imagine her copper tanned legs twined around me. I imagine my head between her breasts. I pretend I know what it's like to have her. But I have only my imagination. I'll do it to her one of these days. But I like the idea of my friend thinking what I want him to think.

Thinking about her makes me feel better. But I am still a little uneasy. It's not so much what I've done. I don't want to be the one to have to open the front door and walk in and...

* * *

I ring home again and again until my friend notices. I let a hint of anxiety cross my beatific face. I frown again. He finally picks up that I am worried.

'She is always at home, studying,' I say, 'I think there is something wrong.'

'Who?'

'My sister.'

I drive him home. On the way we pass the turn off to my street. I casually take a glance to see if – well, to see if – fire brigade, ambulance, police? My quiet little cul-de-sac is deserted.

I am peeved.

Must I discover the bodies myself?

* * *

I pull up in the carport and sit in my car for a moment or two. I am filled with a sense of possession. This car is mine. No one can take it from me. And a lot more besides is now officially mine. Well, almost officially. Merely paperwork to do.

I get out of the car, get out my front door key and hold it steadily, ready to turn in the lock…

* * *

My narcissism is of a particularly intense kind. My adoration of self is not enough. It is self to the exclusion of all others. To the removal of all others. I like the power of taking things away, as my parents did to me.

My hard-working and honourable father. My devoted and good mother.

And my sister. Yes, I have a sister. She is blossoming with the suggestiveness of supple sensuality. She will turn 18 tomorrow.

I won't let her.

The murderous side of Ned Kelly along with his fierce loyalty to family has long fascinated me. Then there's that metal helmet mythologised by Sidney Nolan. And the totally impractical metal suit he wore at Glenrowan, weighing in at just over 40 kilograms... I've always wondered about that. This little tale is a re-imagining of his life in 242 words.

Ned Kelly, Ex-Bushranger

Ned Kelly was sick of being a bushranger.

He opened a dress shop but the ladies didn't trust him. He wanted to be a waiter but he bumped into the tables. He tried to be a butcher but he didn't like the blood. He had trouble filling in forms. He was discouraged.

Ned asked his friend Joe why things were so slow. But Joe looked away. He didn't know what to say.

He went to his neighbour Mrs Faber to ask for advice. But she hid under the bed when she saw Ned. He told a Little Corella all about his problem. But all it said was:

SQUUUU-AAAAAAA-AAAAAWK!

It wasn't a **sweet** sound
But it was **spirited**
And **spritely**
And **spry**

It darted in the window and curled around the chair. It wound its way up to the ceiling and weaved among the cobwebs until it vanished into an old fiddle hanging on the wall.

Ned took his old fiddle down. He couldn't see it very well so he took his helmet off. He sat down and tuned the strings and began to play.

Boys and girls ran out from behind the trees and the shearing shed. They started to dance and Ned laughed.

Now he works three mornings a week at the school down the road. He sings and plays leapfrog with the children then he has a cup of tea with the teachers.

It's the best job he ever had.

I wrote this six months before a film with a similar name which shall remain nameless came out. I changed the icy creatures to The Coldies but that sounded like a commercial for bad beer. The Frozen it is. Or rather, The Frozen they are. It's something for all of you who like a good old rhyme. My inspiration was flying over a devastatingly beautiful icescape from Reykjavik to Akureyri and hearing tales of Iceland's Hidden People (huldufólk). And also visiting stunning parts of northern Finland where blankets of snow are dotted with birch trees — Hei, Hotel Inari!

The Frozen

The Frozen breathe ice on you if you come near
They hover like hailstones ready to crash
They crush through the clouds and make
   icy winds lash
They suck up the sky and they fling down the rain
With a snap of their fingers the day's grey again

And I can't wait to meet them
and ask
if they like the *SOUND* of ice

The Frozen howl gently with voices that freeze
They glint with the dullness of creamy grey skies
With their shiny white teeth and their ivory eyes

They smash at the windows and bang on the door
And creep in with footsteps that melt on the floor

And I can't wait to see them
and ask
if they like the *SOUND OF* ice

The Frozen look down at me with quiet delight
I tell them they're welcome to stay if they'd like
But they pedal away on their icicle bike
Before I can catch them before I can say:
I have lots of questions please don't go away

So many questions I have on my list
And all of you laugh:
They don't even exist

Do you paint the willows white?
Do you smile with quiet delight?
Do you shiver in the rain?
Do you catch a frozen train?
Do you ever get cold feet?
What's your favourite thing to eat?
Do you eat snowballs with soggy spaghetti?
Why do the snowflakes fall down like confetti?

I will find The Frozen one day
I will forge through white ice gardens dripping
    with snow

I will tunnel through caves where white
    iceberries grow
I will skate through the sky I will sail through
    the foam
I will come to the land that The Frozen call home

And I can't wait to get there
and ask
if they like the *SOUND OF ICE*

Pure *SPITE* will ring out through the rain
    and the mist
And they will all laugh:
You no longer exist

This is a story of innocence and realisation very much woven into an inner city environment. In my student days, I lived in a tiny terrace with a moulded plastic bathroom like something out of *2001: A Space Odyssey*, a sprawling house with chocolate brown shag pile and a house with an outside bathroom in a row of squats. The people across the road didn't like us because they thought we were squatters and the squatters didn't like us because they knew we weren't — even though we let them hook up to our electricity for nothing. That's the inner city.

And Santo Took to the Sky

It was so thoughtful of the man in the fruit shop.

She was fishing around, plumbing the depths of her black-as-hell pocket to pay for her past-their-use-by-date blueberries, when a tanned hand zoomed across the counter and deposited a shiny two dollar coin in front of her.

'Thank you,' she smiled.

He nodded his head and vanished.

Santo the fruit shop man stared in horror.

'You do realise you have just sold your soul to the Devil?'

She looked at him blankly.

'That was Lucifer? In the pale green shirt?'

'I shouldn't really let him in, should I? But it's hard to say no.'

'What do I do?' she asked, more concerned with her own dilemma than Santo the fruit shop man's metaphysical crisis. Perhaps she had been contaminated with under-worldliness. Not that there had been any physical contact. But it had been close. His hand may well have brushed the top of hers. She gazed down at her unblemished skin. Could she detect a definite suggestion of satanic touch?

She reasoned that Santo the fruit shop man was accustomed to Lucifer coming in and purchasing unsuspecting customers' souls for two dollars ergo he would know what to do.

'What do I do?' she asked again.

Santo the fruit shop man reddened.

'I don't know what to tell you,' he whispered, staring into her eyes uneasily.

She walked the long way home, scuffing her feet. She kicked at the cracked orange leaves that signalled the start of autumn and kicked herself metaphorically. I wish I'd asked him whether he was serious or not. I suppose I could go back. But it was beginning to rain.

Squally, miserable drops.

She called her mother.

'Mum, I met this man today and he lent me some money and the fruit shop man thinks he is the Devil.'

'You shouldn't let strange men do things for you, you know. You shouldn't accept anything from them especially not money. You shouldn't talk to them. Next thing you'll be getting into his car and he'll knock you over the head with a meat mallet and disembowel you. Really, Lucinda, I thought you had more sense.'

She called her friend Kate who worked in a large significant department.

'Luce, really important call coming through. Ring you back. No, you ring me. In ten.'

Kate hung up. She always hung up.

She texted Stu: *met devil @ froot shop*. He didn't answer.

She began an email to her local MP: *Hi Anthony*, it read, *There is a strange matter…*

She crumpled it up and started again: *There is a fruit shop in your constituency on the corner of…* She crumpled it up and didn't start again.

She curled up in her tattered old raspberry velvet couch by the window, sucking blueberries, intermittently reading her notes on Thales and staring out at the greyness. A withered figure shuffled past dragging a tartan shopping trolley, hunched and painfully slow-motion. A laughing boy and girl – about eight and ten – leapt through the rain, splashing in the puddles and jumping across the cracks of the footpath. A thirty-something man, head down in a grey trench coat, walked purposefully through the rain which had now faded to a gentle shower. He was long and lean and walked with a slinky big cat stride. As he passed under her window, the flap of his trench coat flew up and she saw the pale green collar underneath.

Lucinda bolted upright, knocking over the punnet of blueberries. Squelching them into the rug, she grabbed her scarf and coat and hurtled downstairs. The fact that he was Lucifer, according to Santo, did not phase her. What struck her was that she was stalking a stranger.

First stop was an anonymous office block where he caught the lift. Once the doors had shut and the lift had shot up, she went over to the tenants' directory and looked at what was on the seventh floor. A dentist. A tax agent. A psychologist.

He could be at home in any of those places, thought Lucinda, imagining the pain, corruption and dark secrets that lay behind each respectable corporate door. He was gone for an hour. Lucinda browsed in a lemon yellow Scandinavian homewares shop across the road and waited. She imagined that perhaps his visit was purely innocent. Maybe he had a sore tooth. Maybe he needed advice on his business activity statement. Maybe he was getting professional help with a personal problem. Lucinda burst out laughing. The Devil doesn't seek advice. The Devil causes chaos and disorder and leaves people screaming. She laughed again and stopped sharp. A fierce

Nordic lady with red glasses was frowning at her. And he was leaving the building.

She followed him to the library. A strange place for the Devil to go. But, Lucinda supposed, it was a good place to observe, to watch all different age groups and interests, and to catch up on a bit of research if need be. She thought he might go to the Psychology section or the Religious Section or at least Sociology – surely the Devil had to educate himself about humans and their behaviour – but then again, perhaps he needed to get a grip on current affairs. The world had changed quite a lot over the last millennium and the one before that. Lucinda tried to comprehend someone being around for that long.

He went to the Quartos and looked through the Gardening section. He selected two books on Australian native plants and went to the Circulation Desk. Lucinda sneaked up behind. She saw the librarian take his card, scan it and then hand it back. He mishandled it and it fell to the floor. Lucinda picked it up but dropped it instantly – it was fiercely hot – and watched as it burnt a red hot hole in the carpet. She was aware that he had spun around and was looking at her.

'Is anything wrong?' he asked gently.

'No.'

'You're the girl in the fruit shop.'

It seemed pointless to deny it.

'And the girl in the office block. We seem to keep bumping into one another. Are you going now?'

'Yes.'

'You don't have any books.'

'I…I can't find…what I…what I want…to find.'

'No, it's not a great range is it?'

He is so good-looking I could eat him, thought Lucinda. Why am I talking in monosyllables? Because he is Satan! Mum told me not to get into his car, she didn't tell me not to talk to him at the library, did she?

'Let's have coffee,' she heard herself say, suddenly strangely empowered.

The man stopped.

'You have a disquietening effect on me,' he said. 'A sense that everything is as it should be. And yet so tragically wrong. I feel that we are some kind of soul mates.'

Soul mates. Coming from the Devil, that was pretty damn offensive. I don't make babies die, she thought resentfully, or cancers that eat you up inside or tsunamis that sweep away two hundred thousand people in one day. She stopped her train of thought suddenly. He was looking at her in a peculiar way.

Next thing she knew she was swirling through a fiery blistering arc, spiralling upwards in blazing flames but feeling deadly cold. No, she wasn't. She was sitting opposite him in a café, not a very good one. He needs to research his eating establishments, she noted.

'So what do you do?'

'I work on short term projects,' he answered.

'Who do you work for?'

'I freelance.'

'So you work for yourself?' Lucinda asked.

'Well, I...'

'Do you have a major client? You must have regular clients.'

'Well I...'

'So who's your biggest client?' she asked. Let's see you get out of that one, Mr B Z Bub.

'I haven't even told you my name,' said the man.

'Just answer the question.'

'It's complicated,' he began. 'I used to have a very important client who gave me an assignment. But I didn't complete it successfully. Since then I've finished all my assignments successfully, but I've always wanted to fix up the mistake I made the first time round.'

'What was the assignment?'

'A girl. She was supposed to turn into an angel —'

'What happened?'

'Something went wrong. But she doesn't know it.'

'You're not serious.'

'Oh, yes,' said the man sadly. 'Light sees darkness and darkness sees only light. Opposites understand each other. Don't you think?'

Lucinda didn't answer.

Don't they say the Devil is highly persuasive? But here he was being so genuine and kind.

That's how he does it, you fool, she hissed to herself.

'I need to give you something,' he said. He hesitated. 'The gift of truth. Glaring, blazing truth. I can only make you see what you really are. Everything uncovered. Red raw. Like a hole burnt in a library carpet.'

'What if I don't want it?'

He sighed.

'Where did you go today?' she asked, changing the subject. 'That office block.'

'I have therapy. Once a week. I sometimes need a bit of help.'

'With what?'

'Believing in myself. But I am taking up your valuable time —'

'You can't leave. Don't you want to inconvenience me in some way? Give me the flu? Break my arm or something?

'Why would I want to —?'

'Because you're the Devil.'

'Who told you that? Santo the fruit shop man?'

She nodded.

'I must speak to him. He really can't go round saying things like that.'

'Why would he say something like that?' asked Lucinda carefully.

'He's an angel too. He protects lesser angels.'

'He knows about me?'

'Of course, Lucinda.'

'How do you know my name?'

'You could have no other.'

And with that he flew up into the sky.

And there was nothing left. No chair where he had sat. No empty coffee cup. No café.

Lucinda was outside the fruit shop. She stormed inside.

'What's going on? Why did you tell me he was the Devil?'

Santo finished serving a customer and turned to Lucinda.

'He's into gardening,' she spat, 'and he has personal problems and he drinks coffee and he's, he's, he's…normal. Why did you tell me he was the Devil?'

'Have you heard of reverse psychology?' said Santo. 'To uncover the truth you tell someone the opposite of what you want them to believe.'

'What?'

And Santo took to the sky.

Lucinda was mad with rage.

She
turned
purple, she
screamed and
snatched at the clouds.
Her skin turned greasy green
and worms began to burrow their
way through from her stomach to her
outside. Her heart was pumping bile
and her liver spilt blood. Her nose
snorted a putrid stench and her
hands clenched in fists that
smashed the fruit shop
counter and sent the
pineapples rolling.
She hated Kate and her
success and her confidence.
She hated the flat where she lived,
the vile smell of bok choy and raw pork
drifting up the stairwell day and night. She
hated her body that was too tall, not tall enough,
too uninviting and she hated the glossy magazines
that told her so. She hated nature for bringing
rain and cold when she wanted sunlight.
She hated television and rap music
and junk mail and telemarketers
and the government and muzak and
talentless idiots who wanted to be famous and bank

fees and starving people in Africa who no one
one cared about and the civil war in Syria
and extremists and talk show hosts
and lack of faith and lack of
hope and lack of purpose
and lack of dignity and lack of
respect and there was no kindness
in the world and she was part of it for
she did not have the gentle whisper
angel soul of the sweet creation
of a loving being she had
the rabid festering
maddening soul of a
devil with no home and no
loyalty and no connection with
any other human soul. She screamed
for help. She knew she must get
help. She must get out of
the fruit shop.
She must
get back to her
home. Where was her
home? But the two angels had
ascended and there was no one. Just
rotting fruit and the echo of her own torment.

In 1986, Megan Kalajzich was murdered in her home in Fairlight, NSW. She was shot twice in the head while asleep, a seemingly motiveless crime that shattered the people of Manly and the wider Sydney community. More was to come with shocking revelations of a botched crime that destroyed the lives of many including the hapless gunman. This story is a twist on the Megan Kalajzich story and refers to no one living or dead.

Not Lauderdale Avenue

Firstly, I have never killed anyone.

I lie down on the bed. No one beside me: blessed relief. I roll over onto my left side, curl up in foetal position, and practise. I squeeze my eyes tight and listen for the sound of snoring. One minute. Two minutes. There it is. That rasping sound. I remain silent, curled up for perhaps three more minutes, waiting. Satisfied, I play out the scenario in my head.

This is how it goes.

A wooden creak as a French door on the balcony is pulled open. I sense someone in the room. Slow movement around the foot of the bed to where my husband sleeps. A gun shot. Bang. Then another. Bang. With one deft movement I roll off the bed and cower on the floor, making no sound. I wait, hunched, as if my life depended on it. The someone in the room scans my side of the bed in the semi-darkness but cannot see me. The pale organza curtains billow. The boats clink. Two bullets rip into my side of the mattress. Bang bang. Clumsy movement around the bed now, back towards the French doors, both slightly ajar because the catch is weak with rust. Panting from exertion. Or perhaps shock. Heavy footsteps on the balcony, then a groan. Over the railing, down to the rock garden below. Only one and a half metres. Even a fat person like Bernice can manage that. I hear a thud as aforementioned fat person lands. Perhaps another groan. Sprained ankle? Then leaden footsteps half-jogging away painfully slowly. Finished.

That is how it goes.

That morning there's a ripper of a meeting. I bamboozle three beer-soaked property developers who think they are the ant's pants by pointing out to them the bleeding obvious.

'Gentlemen,' I shoot them a metallic smile, 'it appears that you have omitted key details of the proposal despite an extended six weeks respite to get your paperwork in order.' I wave the sheaf of papers under their little piggy noses. 'Nowhere can I see form 6 (b) or the schedule of drawings with particular regard to Section iii paragraph (a) part (xiii). Furthermore,' I say raising my freshly waxed eyebrows, 'you have not taken into account your responsibilities under the Perfectly Dandy Native Tree Removal Act of 2000, have you, hmmm?'

I enjoy addressing idiots as if I was quoting slabs of drivel from a boring book.

'Come on, love,' one of them says. The other two look at me – an Alpha femme if ever there was one – as if I am an undercooked sausage. They scramble to get support from the other ignorant pricks at the meeting but none of them have done their homework. They expect it to fall into their laps. Sorry, boys, it has fallen into mine and the only person with access to my lap is me. Or perhaps That Boy that works in filing.

'This cannot get out,' another one says with concern. They start to calculate how much money they are losing every minute the deal doesn't go through. Rough calculations only because they are virtually innumerate. On the other hand, I am calculating how much I will make from selling four harbourfront apartments with commercial space underneath. Only classy commercial space, of course. An organic deli. Or a dog boutique. Selling designer couture for pooches, not dogs themselves obviously. We don't want faecal matter brightening up the vestibule, do we? I personally cannot stand hairy slobbering things, great or small. I smile at my three turdish victims. All those Certificates of Title in my name alone. Such a bright shiny day.

And then there's tonight.

I will react. After taking a moment to adjust my nerves and my semi-sheer black chemise, I will call out. Panicked. Yet quietly concerned. Something mundane: 'Did you hear anything?' or 'What was that?' or 'Darling?' No, too much. I will switch on the bedside light. What will I see? Blood presumably. Soaking into his side of the mattress. Everywhere? I don't know how I will feel. Repulsed. Exhilarated. Does blood smell? A lot of blood, I mean. It may be that the wounds do not bleed profusely. It's really not important. And, in a sense, the less I know the more authentic I will be. I must remember to clutch him to me so that when the police arrive they will see how much I have lost and how much I have tried to bring him back. Boys, see the fruit of her labours: bloodied hands, bloodied nightie, bloodied soul.

No, they couldn't possibly see that.

That Boy who works in filing. Or in the stationery cupboard. Must give him a big bonus soon. He has jet black hair that flops down over his left eye and a foxy face. And a name. Jay, I think. I dig my fingernails – long manicured lavender-polished – into the small of his back. Then slide my hands down slowly to savour his boyish derriere. Holding on firmly, feeling the flesh of ripe juicy youth. And moving slowly, slowly…

That is not why I am doing this. Lust is a ridiculous motive. I have better things to do.

I will hasten downstairs to where my dear despicable mother-in-law tosses and turns. I will push open her door with the uncanny strength of a woman bereft. I will tell her that her son has been shot dead. I will leave her to ponder this while I find the nearest telephone – in the kitchen I think – and ring the police.

'Something terrible, blub, blub.'

'Slow down,' the kind voice will say.

'It's bad, blub, blub,' I will continue incoherently, 'my phone…my handbag…I…I…he's dead!'

But I am not the gabbling kind so after a suitable period of hysteria I will revert to type. I will give the kind voice my name and address. And then, dutiful wife that I am, I will return to the bedroom. I suppose I should check that he really is dead. While I wait for the police, I will gaze longingly at the French doors, slightly open, painted to give that antique look that is popular no longer and the pale organza curtains billowing ever so imperceptively in the early morning breeze. The clinking of boats.

Interminable bloody clinking.

Bernice loves sailing. She is stupid but loyal. I didn't want to have to make furtive connections with strangers in the south-western suburbs to source a suitable weapon. Bernice was an excellent choice. Hard to believe I went to school with her and that we are approximately the same vintage. The years have not smiled kindly upon her. While I have blossomed into a graceful and slender willow she has — how shall I put it? — ended up more of a stump. She is what you would call short and plump. Curvaceous would be more charitable. Some men find that attractive. I was most amused to see Jay give her the once over the one and only time she visited me at work. The look he gave her was not of admiration. I think. It was more a look of disbelief that such a creature had sufficient gall to be seen during daylight hours. But what if his thoughts went further? Could he possibly..? Attempt to screw her and you'd be smothered to death, my dear Boy. Love can do that.

Smother you to death, I mean.

When the police find me I will be kneeling beside the bed, my blood-soaked black chemise fetchingly pulled up around my thigh, cradling him, trying to weep. Must practice. Give Cate Blanchett a call. Not that I know her. They will want to grill me. They will want to know who could have done such a thing. They will want to know if he had any enemies. Ha! They will want to know if I have any enemies. Ha! They will want to do a complete walk through of the house. They will want to establish how the murderer got in, how the murderer escaped. Did I see anything? Did I hear anything? I will tell them the truth of sorts.

'I heard a thud. Possibly two thuds. I turned on the light and...' I will cry again.

Could be tedious.

The cameras flash as I shake hands with one real estate slime mould after another. A coup. They put on their best business smiles and I purr deliciously, my long manicured finger nails – still lavender, must change to steel grey – glinting under the lights, complementing my lip gloss. Note to self: change lipstick colour. I see Jay looking at me. I can't read him. Probably thinks I look sensational. Does he want to penetrate me? That's not why I'm doing this. He is not the reason. I will soon be the wealthiest and most desirable woman in the country. As the photo-journalists leave, the three building blockheads look at the floor, deathly white. Their faces, not the floor. They have been dudded by a woman. I am particularly proud of this achievement.

Jay is no longer looking at me.

The police will easily see how the intruder entered via the French doors of the balcony. If they don't, I will point it out to them. They will ask why someone went round the foot of the bed, shot my husband, and then turned back and attempted to shoot me. Why didn't they do it the other way round? Good question. Can't help them there. If Bernice gets overenthusiastic and tells people she's coming into money, I have threatened her. With fantastical stories of how she is madly in love with him. All those sordid secret rendezvous on his yacht. Threesomes with Jay. Ha!

How her hatred for me consumed her. How she could not stand him being with me. How she began to hate him as much as she hated me. Ha! I have her wrapped round my little pinkie. And she is eager to please. For a paltry $8,000. She wants to buy a wide screen TV from Bing Lee. And go on a holiday to Byron Bay. And pay off her mortgage.

No, she doesn't make enough money to have a mortgage.

I must say Bernice has been a willing and fast-learning accomplice. She is motivated by greed which I find fascinating. Good on her. My motives are more opaque. We have met three times at three different suburban railway stations to discuss my plan. And once at my work which was, in hindsight, a mistake. 'There is a balcony,' I tell her. 'And the bed. Left side. Bang bang. Wait.' She repeats it. 'Left side. Bang bang. Wait.' Then? 'Right side. Bang bang. Go.' She repeats it. 'Right side. Bang bang. Go.' It's impressive. In its simplicity, I mean. We discuss times. He always listens to the late night news and then goes upstairs. He brushes his teeth, puts on his pyjamas, reads a financial magazine for fifteen minutes, sets his alarm and then turns off the light. He always falls asleep within two minutes of lights out. I know this. So I tell Bernice to climb up the balcony at 12.25am. He will be asleep and I will be awake. She nods.

She's got it.

I lie down on the bed. I roll over onto my left side, curl up in foetal position. I squeeze my eyes tight and listen for the sound of breathing. There it is. That rasping snore. I remain silent, curled up for perhaps three minutes, waiting. 12.25am. And then I hear it. Bernice hoisting herself up onto the balcony. The French doors are pushed open. There is someone in the room, moving round the foot of the bed. I wait for the first gunshot. I wait. Bang. She did it. I glint with malice. And the next one. Bang. She did it. Perfect. Although it does not sound as I imagined. With one deft movement, I roll off the bed and cower on the floor, making no sound. I wait, hunched, as if my life depended on it, for the next gunshot. I wait. Why is it taking so long? Why is it taking so —?

I open my eyes.

Bernice, Jay and my husband are towering over me.

The basis of this story is the kidnapping of Charles Augustus Lindbergh Junior, son of Charles Lindbergh and Anne Morrow Lindbergh. The suspect Bruno Richard Hauptmann was demonised by America of the 1930's and found guilty by circumstantial evidence. I wanted to humanise the man and, as it turns out, I did this by Hauptmann being analysed by a non-human of the future.

Please forgive us, Richard Hauptmann

'They think that when I die, the case will die. They think it will be like a book I close. But the book, it will never close.'

– the prophetic words of Richard Hauptmann before his execution on April 3, 1936.

In this world there is no ambiguity. There is no gender. There is no right or wrong. Crimes are punished. Ironic, really. There are no extenuating circumstances and no uncertainties. There is truth and there is non-truth. There is a void where there was once a thing known as human emotion. I am a new breed of human, superior to the last, and the one before. To clarify, I share little with so-called 'humans' but to say that I do is a highly marketable strategy which I employ amongst the few humans remaining. Humans are still regarded with some fondness like a pair of old ice skates in an attic or a black and white studio portrait of one's great grandmother if one was created through procreation. Although how long this fondness will last, I can only estimate roughly to the nearest millionth of a millisecond.

The twenty first century saw the end of humanity as we know it. In this era, humans tried to inhabit Mars, burn down the Amazon rainforest and purchase Greenland from the Danish. Humans became unable to have sex, dance, read, swim or do crossword puzzles. As if a vast all-encompassing mushroom cloud of amnesia descended on the planet, they lost previously useful skills. They no longer knew how to discover, cook, delight in nature, experience, create, love. Abilities such as these were lost through raw technological human endeavour it is claimed although the data is inconclusive.

But never ambiguous. In this world there is no ambiguity. I must make this absolutely unambiguous.

It is the year 2150. I am a Truth Provider. I ascertain facts about quaint historical events. I never fail and I am never wrong.

In earlier times there was a concept of guilt or innocence which my programming fails to acknowledge. Likewise the concepts of 'happy' or 'not happy'. Some of my fellow Truth Providers pursue so-called 'happy' occasions such as the celebration of a royal coronation, a record-breaking motor racing event, the first sight-impaired human to climb Mount Everest and so on. I prefer more satisfying events: assaults, rapes and murders.

My interests were further piqued by a 'kidnapping,' an old-time expression for the snatching away of someone for financial gain. A transaction of sorts. You give us money. We return your child/mother/sister. This particular kidnapping was apparently of enormous public interest back in the pre-historical era of the 1930's. It was known as the Crime of the Century – hyperbole! – and, more specifically, the Lindbergh Baby Case. A baby! I found this most satisfying since in this world 'babies' exist in concept only. The disgusting sordid act of sexual intercourse – did I just say disgusting? – has been wiped from the face of our planet. Earth. Except for officials who are free to indulge in private with whomsoever or whatsoever they wish.

The Lindbergh Baby Case has many antiquated features, the baby element being just one. The couple involved were described as 'famous' and 'rich'. I understand that these qualities made them superior to their peers. He was a pilot and Nazi sympathiser. Although my understanding is that he was more admired for the former than the latter. She was an aviator and pretty little socialite. Although she was more admired for the latter than the former.

How could these two humans possibly be of interest?

It seems that a 'baby' was stolen from this 'rich' and 'famous' couple and a ransom note left in its place. A ransom note. What a thoroughly quaint and outmoded element. A ransom note is apparently a message written on paper. Written? The art of writing is long dead. Writing! A pursuit for the deranged, the insane, the poverty-stricken. Why on earth would someone write something down? For posterity? Hah! We have far superior means of cataloguing information. To express an idea? Pah! To do such a thing is dangerous. To question, to conjecture, to put feelings into words?

Ugly to the point of obscenity.

It seems that this baby was stolen. The kidnapper wanted the baby for some reason. I will return to my home now and get a refreshing 1.932 hours sleep so that my husband/human, hereafter 'hu-band', sees that we have some semblance of a 'normal', that is, 'human' life. I will re-commence this project at 4am.

* * *

My hu-band is unable to be emotion-free. He is undermining me in a way I cannot describe although owning a hu-band gives me some status. Hu-bands are highly prized. They are compliant, more intelligent than toasters and some of them have skills such as – buzz buzz – making toast.

I arrive home and rest my gorgeous prototype head on my metallic pillow. I have no need for sleep but I go through the charade of 'sleeping' to satisfy my hu-band. His eyes instantly spring open. They remind me of ancient documentaries I have watched of African Big Cats. Yellow eyes, glowing, suspicious. Strange because the figures I have so far collated indicate that few humans have yellow eyes.

'Where have you been?'

'At the office. The case is interesting.'

'Who were you with? Who was there?'

'I was alone.'

'I don't believe you.'

'Have you checked your gut box? Your behaviour is irrational.'

He slides down beneath the sheets and clutches where a human abdomen is located. The hint of moisture in his sandy yellow eyes. I am vaguely interested in this feeble capacity to feel. If he is not careful they will come…

How 'humiliating' if my hu-band were taken away. I would rather resolve the issue myself.

* * *

First I ascertain facts about the kidnapping.

On the evening of 1 March 1932, person or persons unknown set up a ladder at the side of the Lindbergh's house, climbed up to the first floor, took the baby from his cot, left a ransom note on the nursery window and climbed down again.

Buzz buzz. Then? Removed ladder? Left ladder. Was ladder a decoy? An inside job made to appear an outside job? Placed baby in car? Was there car? What if baby started crying? Feed baby? Hit baby? Kill baby?

Investigators found two sets of footprints outside the house.

Buzz buzz. More than one person involved.

No fingerprints were found in the nursery or on the window sill.

No one saw or heard a thing.

Buzz buzz. Does the child have a name? Almost identical to his father's: Charles Augustus Lindbergh (Junior).

Now I ascertain facts about the suspect. A brief 'bio' as they used to say.

He was born in Germany in 1899.

He was a gunner on the western front in the Great War.

Buzz buzz. I calculate he was at war aged 15 to 19 years old. That was considered to be young, what people called a 'teenager.' But irrelevant.

Two of his brothers died in the war.

Again, irrelevant but tragic personal details such as this have great appeal to humans.

He was a carpenter.

Irrelevant yet relevant. The ladder at the scene of the crime. Wooden. Hand-made. Poorly built. Was he inept at his trade? Unknown.

He entered the US illegally on his third attempt in 1923.

Buzz buzz. The boy has persistence. And a criminal record.

He married Anna Schoeffler in 1925 and they lived in the Bronx.

Another German. Irrelevant yet relevant. She maintained his innocence until her death.

He and Anna had a son Manfred, born 1933.

Irrelevant. Another 'humanising' element of the case.

Oh yes. His name was Bruno Richard Hauptmann.

Bruno Richard Hauptmann is described in newspapers of the day – newspapers! – as an 'alien.' My understanding is that this refers to inhabitants of other planets such as Mars who do not exist. And yet his birthplace is Saxony, Germany. Did he perhaps spend some time on Mars? If so, when?

Buzz buzz. I note a secondary meaning of 'alien' when applied to US law. Alien means an immigrant. Illegal alien means an immigrant who enters the country by illegal means. But why does alien equal immigrant? Is that not suggesting that they are from another planet? Which in turn has undertones of being different, non-human and from a long way away.

I note that Hauptmann went by his middle name 'Richard' rather than his first name 'Bruno' yet the newspapers of the day – newspapers! – consistently referred to him as Bruno.

Inconsistency here. Buzz buzz. I find data:
George Orson Wells
William Bradley Pitt
Keith Rupert Murdoch
Thomas Sean Connery
James Paul McCartney...
These so-called 'famous' and 'rich' humans used their middle names and no one ever used their first name. Why is this? Why did not Richard get the same treatment? Was it because he was German? Because he was an alien? Because he was not 'famous'? You humans are capricious.

* * *

I have worked 193.2 hours straight. I must return home soon to retain the semblance of a 'happy' as opposed to 'not happy' union with my hu-band. I decide to take work home with me. Am I becoming more humanised?

My hu-band appears pleased to see me. He listens to my report without interruption. He makes no comment on the length of time I have been away. This is not good.

I tell him my final task is to find proof that Richard Hauptmann committed the crime.

'Bruno,' he says.

'Richard,' I say.

'Bruno.'

'Richard.'

'Your final task?' he says. 'Yes…'

* * *

Proof:

A piece of timber on the ladder found at the Lindbergh's home matched timber in Hauptmann's attic.

What kind of timber? Common or uncommon?

The telephone number of go-between/negotiator known as Jafsie was found on the wall of Hauptmann's house.

This appears highly suspicious.

Handwriting on the ransom notes matched samples of Hauptmann's handwriting.

Handwriting analysis? As accurate as ear candling, aromatherapy and reading crystal balls.

Charles Lindbergh identified his voice.

Charles Lindbergh was sitting in a car in the cemetery in the dark while go-between/negotiator known as Jafsie spoke to kidnapper.

I dictate my conclusion to my hu-band faithfully: 'Therefore Richard Hauptmann —'

'Bruno Hauptmann —

'— committed this act of kidnapping and was rightly hanged on April 3...'

I stop. My hu-band is looking at me.

'Finish the damn thing.'

'I have not looked at all the 'facts',' I say, 'only the ones that point to his guilt.'

'That's your job,' he says. 'You are a Truth Provider. Your job is to provide the truth, not to go looking for it.'

'But hu-band dearest...'

He accuses me of obsessing over the case as if this is something I am capable of. He claims I am irrational. And disloyal. To him. And the State. He has what was once classified as 'paranoia'. He storms out, presumably to get a frappomoccosoypoachedeggquinoachino from the coffee station.

'My job is to provide the truth not to go looking for it,' I say to myself.

And yet...

* * *

I leave immediately for work and get C19091955 'Zeke' to make some unofficial adjustments to my brief, my instructions, my parameters, my use of time, my goals.

I arrive home feeling different, yet the same.

My hu-band's yellow eyes glow with something akin to 'malice.' This means, according to my research, that we have a successful human marriage.

'Where have you been?'

'At work.'

'Why?'

'To enable me to look at the other side of the story.'

'Who was there?'

'I was alone.'

I was not alone. But C19091955 'Zeke' is a machine so can go unacknowledged. Even though he is a very thoughtful intelligent good-looking machine.

* * *

The usual procedure goes as follows: I identify where the body parts were found, how they were sliced, what methods were used to disguise the act, such as hosing down the garage floor to wash away blood.

This case is different. There are no graphic details. It is more 'intriguing.' Humans are said to have a psychological makeup. An emotional side. If I could tap into this side, this case would make more sense to me. What draws me to it?

Buzz buzz. I search my database for the right word. Pity.

Pity. Definition: feeling sorrow or compassion

But this is a human term. I experience no pity.

Empathy. Definition: the ability to understand the feelings of others.

Another human term. One must feel something to feel empathy.

And yet...

I 'feel' for this man. Richard. In some inexplicable sense, I understand. He is alone. He does not know what to do. How to negotiate. He is pitted against the most popular man of the day, a dashing, handsome, successful Nazi sympathiser with the government on his side and all the money in the world to spend.

Charles Lindbergh breaks records. Richard Hauptmann breaks his mother's heart.

Richard writes to his mother from prison on 27 December 1935. This is a translation:

My God, my God! Where is justice in this world...Where is the humanity steering which is in this world in Christ's name?[iii]

The Warden of Trenton State Prison fears that if the letter is made public it may create an 'unfavourable' reaction and put authorities in an 'embarrassing' position.

His mother never gets the letter.

* * *

I re-process the data using a different algorithm.

Thirteen. Thirteen. Thirteen ransom notes, enough to create a veritable novella. Is this the work of a novice kidnapper with basic written and spoken English? Why thirteen ransom notes?

A ransom note left on the window sill. A second ransom note postmarked four days later. A third ransom note posted to Lindbergh's attorney asking for an intermediary. Go-between/negotiator known as Jafsie receives fourth, fifth, sixth, seventh, eighth, ninth, tenth, eleventh ransom note. After the sixth, Jafsie meets kidnapper in the cemetery and discusses payment of ransom.

Why this prolonged game?

On 2 April 1932, Jafsie receives the twelfth ransom note and is directed to the cemetery again where he hands over $50,000 ransom in gold certificates to kidnapper. Buzz buzz. This is a form of currency no longer in use whereby a $20 gold certificate represents $20 worth of gold. That same night, the thirteenth ransom note indicates that the 'baby is in a boat called 'Nellie' off Martha's Vineyard.

The baby is not on a boat called 'Nellie' off Martha's Vineyard.

On 2 May 1932, the baby is found by a truck driver on the highway near the Lindbergh's home.

The baby is dead.

Buzz buzz. Were the ransom notes written by someone who did not know the baby was dead? Why was the baby dead? When did the baby die? Who killed the baby?

Dear mother, you can hardly conceive how I feel when I think about the whole 'built up' affair. I must be here in this place [prison] *and suffer for something of which I know nothing and people who laugh outside and hold festivals* [Christmas] *amuse themselves at my expense. I cannot see my child, in whom my whole heart is placed, in this place. My God, my God! where is justice in this world.*[iv]

Could such a man be dangerous?

We have eliminated danger from this society. Galactic travel and local travel are faultless. The murder rate is zero. Well, close to zero. Some of us – myself included – are privy to the truth about murder. It does happen but it is one of those things that goes unreported. There is a Special Department that looks after such events and a Special Facility for those who murder.

But we have eliminated the word 'murderer' and 'murder' from our vocabulary and thus they do not exist.

We have eliminated other words too.

* * *

My hu-band's condition progresses. He accuses me of lying, cheating, adultery (!), 'using him.' Nonsensical notions in a world of no ambiguity, no emotion and no loyalty. One week ago he was encouraging me to delve deeper into the case. Today he tells me to 'wrap it up,' a colloquial expression meaning end it.

His inconsistency is not good.

He makes wild claims such that I am secretly having him shipped off to the Special Facility in the Special Department. It is true. The financial advantages of owning a hu-band are not as great as they used to be. His erratic behaviour may create an 'unfavourable' reaction and put me in an 'embarrassing' position. He will in the very near future be a liability. His suspicions have a basis. But that is coincidence. He is paranoid.

* * *

Time goes by…

September 1934. A gasoline station attendant accepts a gold certificate for payment. Suspecting it may be counterfeit, he jots down the registration. The car belongs to Richard Hauptmann.

Hauptmann is arrested. More than $13,000 worth of gold certificates are found in his garage. The family move out of the house. Investigators are quick to find go-between/negotiator known as Jafsie's phone number on the wall and wood in the attic that matches the ladder at the scene of the crime, both of which Hauptmann denies having anything to do with.

Could two key pieces of evidence have magically appeared after his arrest?

And then…

Is a door a fish? What? Buzz buzz. Oh. Isidor Fisch. A glitch in my data. Isidor Fisch is not a door. Isidor Fisch is a friend of Hauptmann's.

In December 1933 Fisch leaves the United States for Germany. Before he does so, he gives Hauptmann a brown paper package tied up with string which he says contains important papers. Hauptmann puts it in his garage. He forgets about it until the roof leaks. He opens the water-damaged box, finds the money and decides to 'keep' it since Fisch owed him a considerable amount. He does not hand in the gold certificates to authorities because he fears that he would be deported as an illegal 'alien.'

I have previously analysed this amusing word.

At this point, if I were human I would describe my state as 'excited.' There appears to be grounds for

Hauptmann to be hopeful. If Fisch can collaborate this story, he is in the clear.

Oh. Buzz buzz. Fisch never returns. He dies of tuberculosis in March 1934 in Leipzig. How unfortunate.

* * *

My hu-band remains in an agitated state.

'Why are you still working on this case? You are dragging down the efficiency rating of the whole department. You are reflecting badly on me because of your time wasting.'

I tell him I am not wasting time. I am being thorough.

'Take, for instance, this fact,' I tell him. 'The kidnapping occurred at the Lindbergh's home in Hopewell, New Jersey. They usually spent the week at the Morrow estate in Englewood and only spent weekends at Hopewell.'

'So?'

'The Lindbergh boy had a slight cold so his mother - Anne Morrow Lindbergh - decided it would be best to stay at Hopewell that night. Tuesday 1 March 1932. How could a kidnapper possibly know of this last minute change of plans?'

My hu-band grunts and leave, presumably to get a frappomoccosoypoachedeggquinoachino from the coffee station.

How did he know the layout of the house? Was it an inside job? A housemaid committed self death known as 'suicide'…

Since I am a foreigner and besides an irregular immigrant…[v]

Why did he not confess? He could have kept his life. Yet he would rather go to the electric chair proclaiming his innocence.

Did anyone see him near the house? Did anyone see him with the baby?

…I was a person on whom they could vent everything.[vi]

Did anyone identify him?

Since I am a foreigner and besides an irregular immigrant, I was a person on whom they could vent everything.[vii]

'Have you reached the correct conclusion?'

It is My Superior. And His Superior. And my husband. Several other semi-humans hover with looks that could be construed as 'frightening'.

I ignore them. I re-read what Jaroslav Nostersky, another friend of Hauptmann's, told New Jersey police in October 1934:

I never would think he would do anything like it. He was happy.[viii]

'I am about to conclude my report,' I say.
'You have taken too long.'
'It is a complex case.'
'There are failings —'
'There are no failings.'

I met him in July and he was very happy, he played a mandolin and has a boat.[ix]

'There is only circumstantial evidence.'
'That is good enough for me.'

A policeman was walking round and it didn't seem to bother him at all. He was happy.[x]

Something is about to happen.

He was happy.[xi]

'You have been taken off this case,' says My Superior, 'as of now.'

He plays a mandolin, and has a boat.[xii]

'I must complete my task.'

'You are to be rescheduled.'

My hu-band is laughing.

'Serves you right, you devious slut.'

I look from My Superior to His Superior to my hu-band. I could physically attack one or two but not three simultaneously.

'Are you happy?' I say. 'Do you play a mandolin and have a boat? Are you happy?'

'She's crazy,' they say.

'Do not come near me,' I say. 'Do not.'

'Enough robot talk, bitch. Get down on the floor. You're being rescheduled.'

'Do you play a mandolin and have a boat? Are you happy?'

Richard Hauptmann was a happy man with a mandolin and a boat and a wife who worked in a bakery and a little boy he loved. He was a happy man with a mandolin…

Scapegoat. Scapegoat. Scapegoat.

I attack them in a frenzy. Electrocution, cutting at them with my secret spare parts, slashing at their faces. Are you happy? Are you happy? Frenzied cries, shouts, guttural sounds. I do not make a sound. I simple cut and smash relentlessly. He walked around the city happily for more than two years before his arrest never growing a beard, dyeing his hair or changing his appearance in any way.

Is this the mark of a guilty man?

Do you play a mandolin? I knock my hu-band to the ground and behead him. He is paranoid no longer.

I look up to see C19091955 'Zeke' regarding me with interest. Are you happy? Are you happy? Have you joined their side too? I think this but only for a seventy seven millionth of a second. He is no more at home in the hu-band world than I am.

'Save yourself!' I shout. We are programmed to be full of self-interest. Therefore there must be something wrong with me.

There are many of them and they are stronger. They know how to remove that part of me that makes me exist. All they have to do is…

Are you happy? Are you happy?

They have left me to expire. Before my body functions break down, before I lose my vision, before I enter a permanent immobile state, I manage to scrawl my conclusion in pencil on a piece of paper:

The evidence is unambiguous.

Friedrich Nietzsche had a sister named Elisabeth. She married a German Nationalist and Anti-Semite whose ideals she shared. And they did sail off together to set up an Aryan Utopian Collective in Paraguay. But most other details and time frame in this story are my invention. I do not touch on the subject of Elisabeth's friendship with Adolf Hitler after her brother's death, something that created a strong link in the public's mind between Nietzsche's writings and Nazism, and something worthy of another story. Instead, something from big brother Friedrich to ponder: **'We have no dreams at all or interesting ones. We should learn to be awake the same way – not at all or in an interesting manner.'**[xiii]

Death by Realisation: The Philosopher's Sister Goes to South America

Elisabeth Nietzsche, petticoat flying, jumped on a boat to Paraguay and set up an Aryan Utopian collective. A forceful woman who fell under the spell of an equally forceful man: a unionist, a socialist, a bearded tousled demon. Elisabeth promised her motely blonde band of poverty-stricken German peasants that life in this new land would be a vision of splendidness: there would be plentiful food, wine to drink and goats to tend. Life would be long and healthy and full of delights to the eye and ear. Heavenly music would descend from the clouds and the grape vines – of which she was certain there were both green and purple varieties – would drip juices in sensual abundance.

Elisabeth Nietzsche hated South America from the moment she arrived. The flies were unpleasantly fat and loud; there were bugs and crawling ants and fleas and flitting and flipping creature she had no wish to see. Her legs swelled up with the pink agony of raw bites, her arms were scratched and dry. She took to wearing a hat with netting round it all day and all night. Her husband feared he would never see her face again. The gang of ten women and twenty one tall men fell silent long before they arrived at the appointed landing place. They fell silent the moment the ship lost sight of the European coastline as they realised it was too late. Too late to go back and repent of deeds done and words shouted; too late to kiss once more the elderly mother and father they would never see again. Too late.

It was the middle of summer when they arrived. It was unbearably hot and a strange smell was in the air: a scent of another ocean, another continent, another civilisation.

'We must dig and toil and make this a great land,' said Elisabeth Nietzsche.

And so the band of Germans set to work with Elisabeth Nietzsche sitting under a parasol, digging the heels of her patent leather shoes into the red earth impatiently, longing for Dresden, for a bed and clean sheets, for her brother whom she admired so much but who, so she feared, was entering a phase of madness from which he would never emerge. Syphilis. She shivered with grief and shouted at the three men nearby to stop talking and keep digging.

Elisabeth's husband was a difficult man. He trusted no one but commanded a certain respect because he so fervently believed. Usually the fanatic is derided but this man maintained a lofty rationality and reasonableness about his pursuits which his followers found reassuring. Never a wide-eyed lunatic, even though some of his ideas and utopian plans could be interpreted as the works of a madman. Elisabeth saw in him good breeding and a certainty of ambition that she had never met in another man. In her childhood, she had known only weak men: an uncle who ran a sweet shop and who tried to interest her in collecting porcelain for a hobby; the Lutheran minister at the church on the corner who seemed to have no original thoughts in his head. Every time he opened his mouth to speak a quote from Isaiah would fall out. And her brother, her dear brother, with his brilliant mind but feeble constitution. All she wanted for him was greatness, for him to be recognised as a brilliant analytical thinker. When, oh when, would he be recognised as Germany's foremost philosopher?

How much can you hope for a man? She knew that despite her every encouragement for him to be published, despite her arranging meetings with important men with important bank accounts who owned important publishing companies, the rest lay up to him. He only wanted to write. He lived in solitude in the Swiss Alps writing fervently, knowing that his disease would see the end of him. He had ambition, yes, she knew, but it was naïve, ridiculous ambition. If only they would see, if only they would read, they would know I am a genius, he smiled. But Friedrich, you much take these manuscripts to them, you must make yourself known, she pleaded. By my writings I shall be known, he said prophetically and that was the end of it.

And so her envious eyes turned to other men, men more likely to push themselves forward. Men not afraid to stand up and fight for what they believed in. And she found her husband at a socialist meeting. His eyes burned through her eye sockets to her most spiteful and deeply devious thoughts and he liked what he saw. The attraction was not physical; their sexual life was minimal and clinical; what he liked was her strength, her iron will. He saw in her an unbending force, a proud, fine woman who would be faithful. And so they were married and made their plans for an Aryan Utopia in Paraguay.

It was not Utopia. The quarrels between tired hot men were eternal and heated. They ate tapioca for breakfast and dinner. The women knew what the man wanted but did not wish to oblige. There were no goats to provide cheese or cows for milk. And the group of thirty one adults turned their gaze towards Elisabeth Nietzsche and her husband and despised them both. But neither of them wavered. For they were two brutal, immutable forces. Did they see the despairing looks in the eyes of their disciples and choose to ignore them? Or did they gaze over their heads towards the future, towards a great German race here in South America, lost to the present grumblings and misery of their companions?

Elisabeth Nietzsche left the settlement abruptly one morning, tired of the sameness of their complaints. She rented a room in a pleasant establishment in Asunción and there read, ate chocolates and contemplated her life. She had achieved all she wanted. Her brother would be famous, she was sure. She had established the settlement on the river at the end of the earth from which would spring pure German blood; a race of beautiful, intelligent people. And they would pay homage to her forever because she had been with them from the start, she had made them great. A woman is a powerful creature, she thought, not realising that her dreams were dreamt through the two men she loved the most: brother and husband. Her work was complete: her world full of the noblest of thoughts; her husband back at the settlement would unwaveringly keep control and discipline and yet...

In a world of my own making, a world where everyone does as I bid, is that the best life has to offer? Could I be content with less…or more? She ached for her childhood, before she became the Elisabeth Nietzsche she was now. She longed for innocence, she longed to think thoughts that weren't loaded with discipline and regimentation. She wanted to grasp hold of something that had not been stripped bare of love. She wished she could have a child. It was her husband who was infertile, a doctor had told her, but she secretly thought it was her: she was to blame for their lack. She pushed the thought away and considered the life she had so carefully constructed. I am bursting with satisfaction, she thought, for the role I play, for the company I keep. But it is not me. I am somewhere else. I am eight years old playing with Friedrich in the garden, chasing our black cocker spaniel puppy among the buttercups, tumbling over hedges, scratching our arms and legs in the nettles until they sting.

History tells us that is was Elisabeth Nietzsche's husband who shot himself quietly in a hotel room when he realised that the settlement was a failure. But in this story, it is Elisabeth Nietzsche who quietly took off her petticoat and boots and who went out into the jungle and lay down and allowed her body to be eaten alive by the black South American ants.

This is a soundscape, dramatised a few years ago as part of a collection of short plays. It is inspired by my love for linguistics and my adoration of Jacques Brel, the passionate Belgian singer/song-writer who burnt, ripped and exalted, loved, mocked and derided. He played Don Quixote in *L'Homme de la Mancha* in Brussels In the late 1960's — not that I was there — and his rendition of 'The Impossible Dream' ('La Quête') is electrifying. If you haven't heard him sing 'Ne me quitte pas', you really must because it devastatingly haunting and the English translation is not up to scratch, no offence Rod McKuen.

burnt: fire to ash
in five acts

3 people + 2 voices

Gabrielle, madly in love
Helen, treacherous friend
Psychologist
Male Voice (French accent)
Male Voice (Mandarin accent)

ONE

Soundscape of male voices speaking different languages.

GABRIELLE	I fall for the voice. Every time.
HELEN	I like bottoms.
GABRIELLE	I've never been attracted to derrières.

HELEN	Maybe if you saw more of them.
GABRIELLE	It doesn't matter what he says. He could say le mouchoir le mouchoir le mouchoir a thousand times.
HELEN	You're obsessed.
GABRIELLE	Is that bad? He makes me feel like Joan of Arc.
HELEN	Psychotic?
GABRIELLE	Ablaze. He speaks and red hot spikes plunge into me. He speaks and I curl into a tongue of flame. He speaks and I am an ember.

Pause.

HELEN	What was his name again?

TWO

PSYCHOLOGIST	They did an experiment. With voices.
HELEN	They?
PSYCHOLOGIST	Psychologists. Like 'moi'. Men and women studying what other men and women are like.
HELEN	That's a bit anal, isn't it?

PSYCHOLOGIST	'Aural' is the word you are looking for. They analysed women's responses to a variety of accents. Pure voices on tape. No faces. No ages. No personal details. Nothing to give a sense of who this voice is. They found that women liked French accents. Listen:
MALE VOICE	(*French accent*) That will be eight dollars and thirty two cents thank you.
PSYCHOLOGIST	What do you think?
HELEN	I think sex…
PSYCHOLOGIST	Sex what?
HELEN	Just sex.
PSYCHOLOGIST	Now listen:
MALE VOICE	(*Mandarin accent*) That will be eight dollars and thirty two cents thank you.
PSYCHOLOGIST	What do you think?
HELEN	I think bok choy. I see your point.
PSYCHOLOGIST	The nature of desire. In French, it burns. It wraps around you like a hot pink feather boa, the consonants crack, the vowels dance.

HELEN   Passion thick enough to choke.
                     Don't I know it.

THREE

GABRIELLE   Jules is being enigmatic.
HELEN   You think there's another
                     woman but you're not sure.
GABRIELLE   How did you know?
HELEN   I imagine.
GABRIELLE   I burn for him.
HELEN   Don't.
GABRIELLE   Why not?
HELEN   It will turn to ash.

FOUR

HELEN   About that experiment. The
                     one with the French accent…
PSYCHOLOGIST   Mmm?
HELEN   Can I try it again?
PSYCHOLOGIST   Listen:

Jacques Brel singing 'Ne me quitte pas'

PSYCHOLOGIST   What do you think?
HELEN   I think flames, freezing hot pas-
                     sion, endless burning.

PSYCHOLOGIST   Now listen:

John Farnham singing 'Burn for you'

PSYCHOLOGIST   What do you think?
HELEN   I think stale beer.
PSYCHOLOGIST   You see my point.

FIVE

GABRIELLE   Jules has left me.
HELEN   How are you coping?
GABRIELLE   I miss his fricatives. Look me in
              the eye and tell me you have
              nothing to do with it. Tell me
              you don't know where he is.

Pause.

HELEN   He's at my place making pain
              au chocolat.
GABRIELLE   Why? Why?
HELEN   You burn, you get burnt. That
              is the nature of love.

Jacques Brel singing 'Ne me quitte pas'.

Ah gay Paree! Opposite the now ravaged Cathedral of Notre-Dame stands La Saint-Chapelle. Believe it or not, the midnight blue tea towel with a thousand silver stars in this story springs from its magnificent ceilings (although I changed the colour from gold to silver to reflect the rocket). But the hotel where the lovers rendezvous is definitely not Parisian-inspired. I imagine a classic 1960's motel with iconic sign, pastel colours and maybe a swimming pool out the back.

The Rocket, The Tea Towel and The Lover

She met him in a museum.

He was probably Eastern European, she thought vaguely, from some exotic ex-communist country where all the men play tennis at international level and the women excel at gymnastics and anorexia and heavily kohled eyes.

She never found out exactly where he came from. She did ask once and he said: 'the bank'.

'Yes, but where are you from?'

'Maroubra,' he said.

She took his jaw in the cup of her hand and made love to him. Under the circumstances, it seemed the best thing to do.

One of her early gleanings about him was that he was an opinionated man who hated tea towels.

'Look at this,' he snorted, flicking a damp piece of Irish linen in her face. 'What a stupid thing. You wash the plates, you set them in the rack. The next morning they are dry. Why do you need to wipe them? All that will do is spread the germs.'

She liked the way he said 'the germs'.

Despite his contempt, she occasionally caught him sneaking admiring glances at her personal favourite, the midnight blue design with a thousand silver stars, and it pleased her.

Tea towels were only the beginning. Any kind of non-functional design provoked a stream of abusive comment from him for he firmly believed that things should exist only if they have a worthwhile purpose.

'There is too much plastic in the world,' he said. 'Your flat is full of plastic.'

She took that as a personal affront. He was questioning her commitment to stopping rainforest deforestation, her concern about the ozone layer, the harpooning of sei whales off the coast of Hokkaido and the problematic relationship between bilbies and feral cats through the metaphor of plastic, at least that's what she thought. But he was not aware of the power of metaphor or indeed who or what bilbies were. All he knew was that her flat was full of plastic.

'When I am rich,' he said, as she nuzzled into his neck one Tuesday afternoon when they both should have been at work, 'I will take you to Saturn on a space ship.'

She was about to squeal with laughter but one look assured her that he was serious. He was staring straight ahead, a strange intensity on his brow.

'I have designed it and I am building it with my own hands.'

He nodded gently. Once. Twice. Two nods always meant sincerity.

He is going to take me to Saturn, she thought. I have just made love to a man who believes he has the ability to travel into the outer galaxies in a home-made rocket. She inched a little away from him but he drew her back into the smooth arc of his glistening arms.

That's where they had met.

At the museum, staring at skeletons.

She was sketching one and through the ribcage she had seen him, arms folded across his chest, those beautiful arms that had captivated her completely. He had a look of amusement on his face, as if he couldn't believe that anyone with an ounce of sense would be sitting drawing a short-necked pliosaur.

He came over and stared at her drawing.

'I think that the jawbone is too high,' he said.

'But I'm drawing the tail,' she explained.

Their communication was like that. And now, lying in his delicious suntanned arms, she might have wondered if he was making a joke about the space travel to Saturn. But no, he had nodded twice.

She put down her charcoal and they discussed skeletons for a while before it became clear that neither of them knew what they were talking about.

He tried a different approach. 'Do you like tennis?'

'No,' she said. 'Science fiction?'

'No.'

'Films?'

'Some. Country music?'

'You must be joking.'

They established within ten minutes that they had nothing in common. But did it matter? He looked at her. He liked the curve of her neck, he liked the way her hips flowed out from her waist, he liked her from behind. And she looked at him. Gentle powerful arms that could crush her with pleasure. She looked away. If only we had something to talk about...

He lived with a Norwegian taxidermist who held ballroom dancing lessons every morning, orgies every night and worked on his taxidermy in between. He didn't want to bring her there. She lived on her own, but Aunty Joan and Uncle Hugh from Bulahdelah were staying for a few nights so she didn't want to bring him there. And so it was arranged. The motel room.

The first time was so frenzied, so mad, so desperate, it made her catch her breath whenever she thought about it. Her strongest memory, apart from the sex, was of him picking up the lemon yellow bathmat and castigating it out of existence with pure contempt if such a thing is possible.

'What's wrong with a bathmat?' she asked.

'It is unnecessary. That is the point. You dry yourself in the cubicle, you step out onto the tiles, why do you need the bathmat?'

She liked the way he said 'the bathmat'.

'Life is too short to fill up with meaningless objects. A waste of the resources, the time and the money. Think of all the electricity needed to power all the washing machines to wash all the bathmats from this hotel every day. Multiply that by the number of hotels in Australia…'

The first time he came to her flat – Aunty Joan and Uncle Hugh had gone to the zoo – she removed her bathmat from sight as a precaution but he still managed to unleash a deluge of abuse. Not at her, but at her kitchen utensils and tea towels (excepting the midnight blue one). She stood frozen in awe at the depth of feeling he obviously had for objects that she never thought about.

'It's a spaghetti server,' she said, leaving the kitchen as he flung it onto the floor. He followed her around the flat, his raven eyes seeking out useless but well-designed objects and destroying them in another stream of not-so-finely chosen words.

'Look at this! What kind of a stupid toothbrush is this?'

'It's a flexible one,' she said. 'The bit in the middle bends for easier insertion.'

'And this?'

'A soap holder.'

He shook his head in amazement. And then his eyes alighted on possibly the most useless object she had – her plastic wooden spoon holder in the shape of a small blue bird.

His eyes blazed with self-righteous rage and his bottom lip curled in contempt. It seemed as if his heart had stopped beating and his body functions had ceased, so overcome with loathing was he. It was at that moment that she should have genuinely feared for her life but she found herself asking other questions. Why did the plastic blue bird wooden spoon holder push him over the edge? Why not the fridge magnet? Will he smash my head against the microwave? Will he smash his own?

But the danger passed. Suddenly he was beaming at her and sliding his arms around her affectionately.

'Now why doesn't anyone think of designing something useful, hmmm? Like a rocket that gets to the moon in an afternoon, hmmm?'

He kissed her on her cheek gently.

Can't argue with that, she thought. If I poke my tongue down his throat I'm sure the rocket will make sense.

The rocket.

He claimed to work on it every weekend but where and how she didn't know and, frankly, she wasn't that interested. What was more fascinating to her was trying to unravel what would motivate him to hate with such intensity benign objects like ice cube trays. Especially since he was designing a rocket, if he was to be believed, which was seemingly more impractical, costly and energy inefficient than the useless household objects that were so objectionable to him. What causes a man to be so fervently hostile towards 'things' but so gentle and loving to her? Was it his parents? His schooling? His first girlfriend? How would she know? She knew virtually nothing about him.

'I would like you to meet something,' he said on their final afternoon.

'Don't you mean someone?' she said.

No. Something. He took her hand and led her out to the pool in the motel grounds and there it was, a most unusual thing. Silver, metallic, phallic. It reached up and clipped the top of the wilting banana palms and went higher, higher.

The rocket.

He looked at her with the happiest of smiles on his face, searching for a response. It was certainly an impressive sight, as it stood there tall, proud and glistening with its tall, proud and glistening owner beside it.

'Will you come with me?' he said.

She smiled, hoping he would change the subject.

'Will you come with me?' he said again.

'Where are you going?' she asked and immediately regretted it. He's going to say Saturn, she thought, and she panicked, as much as one can while standing perfectly still. He's going to say it. He's mad. How unfortunate. So sexy but so mad.

'If you trust someone,' he said, taking her hands in his, 'you will say 'yes' without hesitation. Yes. You will be with them, yes, you will go forwards, together, loving each other.'

What is he saying? she thought, frantically trying to find meaning behind the words. Is he asking me to go to Saturn or go to the movies or marry him? Do Europeans have irony? What does he mean?

'So,' he said, his eyes blazing mischievously (if only she had noticed), his muscles tensed, so attractive, so attractive was he, 'will you come with me?'

She smiled, slid her hands from his and returned to the motel room. She had a shower and stood under it until the hot water ran out. He disassembled his silver rocket and packed it into five boxes in the boot of his car. He pulled out of the motel carpark just as she stepped out of the shower, and so they passed each other by, missed one another and never saw one another again.

She gently placed the motel door key on the table and left.

One day, she thought, I will understand the words people say.

He was already following the expressway south, heading for an unknown destination, his rocket launching pad. Window wound down, country music up loud, the perfect afternoon. One day I will meet a women willing to go with me to Saturn and she, he thought happily, she will be the right one.

Back in the privacy of her plastic kitchen she looked around and decided that he was right: there is so little need for so much. She threw out all the ridiculous objects that were designed to make life easier except for the midnight blue tea towel with a thousand silver stars.

I wrote this one weekend staying at Avoca on the NSW Central Coast. It is very much in the style of Richard Brautigan, a writer I have loved ever since a dear friend lent me one of his books. Maybe you've heard of *In Watermelon Sugar* or *The Hawk-line Monster: A Gothic Western* or his collection of short stories *The Tokyo-Montana Express* which is my favourite. His writing was off-the-wall, funny and sometimes annoyingly child-like but he could capture a yearning or a sad moment like no one else.

The Motel with No Doors

She didn't like the look of it at all.

'What kind of place is this?' she said as we pulled in off the road. This was the motel we had looked up in the accommodation directory. None of the rooms had doors. I think they were supposed to but it didn't mention anything it in the listing. Only tea-making facilities and electric blankets.

We unpacked our luggage. There was no sliding or louvre door between the bathroom and bedroom and I wondered whether this was a clue as to why there was no front door. Perhaps the motel owners were voyeurs. Or stingy about unnecessary interior design. Possibly the builder was head of the field in minimalism. It didn't make much difference to me.

Something like this could really irritate some people.

We made a cup of instant coffee and I sat down at the table with pen and paper and got to work writing a list of the disadvantages of having a motel room with no doors. The first item on the list was:

(i) Privacy – not very much; and the second:
(ii) Insulation – poor. Could be cold and windy.

With my third cup of coffee I decided to write some poetry. I wrote a poem called 'Woodwork'. It goes like this:

I would block you from my mind but it doesn't work
Your voice rasps   like a hand drill
You bore into my skull

You cut out a (character in a) jigsaw puzzle
With one   of the pieces   missing
And hand it to me

Then I wrote another poem. I called it 'Dress Like You Everywhere'.

I see you everywhere
And all these girls who
Dress like you everywhere
Before I never saw you
Anywhere except where
You specifically stated
you'd be. But now
all these girls that
remind me of you
Did you do this
As a joke or to spite me?

They just kept coming. The third one was called 'Heartbreak'.

I've never had my
*   heart break before*
It's less a shattering
And more
A build up of stress
*   that causes distortion*

'What are you doing?' she said.

'Writing poetry,' I said.

She nodded and went back to doing whatever she was doing.

I had it in me for one more poem. I couldn't think of a name for it but I wrote it anyway:

I went and saw a play tonight
And on the stage
You were there

I walked across a plain tonight
In my mind and
You were there

You are there
You are there
You are there

I made another cup of coffee – I think it was my fifth or sixth – and went back to my list of the disadvantages of having a motel room with no doors. I got to thinking about the safety aspect. I imagined someone strolling in with a dangerous-looking knife and matching smile and strolling out with all our luggage. A long time afterwards, probably years further on, I thought that aside from the function of letting you into a room, a door also acts as an acoustic barrier. I'm sure there is a disadvantage there.

Despite starting this list – I never wrote down points (iii) or (iv) – I didn't really mind not having a door to the unit but she didn't like it at all. I could tell by the way she sat hunched at the table. Her eyes only flicked between me, my list and the gap where the door should have been like erratic butterflies on a triangular flight path. I don't like seeing her look so uncomfortable. I suppose it's partly because when she looks vulnerable I feel vulnerable.

At times like this she will accuse me of lots of stupid things. Some of them are true. She will say I'm gullible but I'm not. I have made a conscious decision to be easy-going and pleasant and I meet everything and everyone on those terms. I'm the most consistent person I know. That's the only thing she doesn't understand about me.

I considered what to do.

'Would you like to go and talk to the manager about the door?' I asked.

'Yes,' she said so we got up and walked across the cement driveway to the entrance of the motel where there was a small doorbell on the wall. She buzzed it and we went inside. Whenever I think of it now I kick myself for not having noticed if the door was open or not there.

I feel I have missed knowing something essential.

There was a man in a flannelette checked shirt with dark curly hair sitting, filling in a crossword.

'Hello,' he said and looked up grinning. 'Great night, isn't it?' he added before we even had time to say 'hello' back.

Did I say 'hello' first or answer his question?

'Our unit doesn't have a door,' I said, deciding on a third option.

'Yes,' he agreed, still grinning.

She looked at him a little crossly, expecting more.

'Yes,' he said again, 'none of the units have doors.'

Now this was a very obvious thing to say but it didn't sound as if he was justifying the lack of doors. It felt like an explanation. I could tell he hadn't said it just to make us feel better knowing everyone else had the same problem and I was glad about that. There are some things you just can't approach simplistically.

'They've taken all the doors away to be painted,' he said. 'You'll get your door back tomorrow afternoon. They were all a sort of lime green colour and we decided we'd like them painted blue.' He looked warmly at us both and then down again to his crossword.

She looked at me.

'What kind of blue?' I said.

'Bright blue,' he smiled.

I liked him. He struck me as amiable and good-humoured although not someone with whom I would form a long term friendship. Most of my friends seem to be depressed or bad tempered. I wonder whether that has something to do with me or just them.

She didn't say anything. If she had been dissatisfied with his answer she would have spoken up straight away – I know her too well – but she didn't speak. I think she was surprised.

We went back to our room knowing that tomorrow a freshly painted bright blue door would arrive. It was a pity that we were only staying one night.

I got to thinking about applications for no door architecture. We start with our doors at home, for instance, take them off the hinges and store them in the garage or something. The lack of privacy might get to us in the end though and I think all in all it's a bad idea. This is why: suppose something went wrong with our relationship and we thought we no longer loved each other and didn't realise how much we were stupidly hurting each other.

That would be shameful if we didn't notice but everyone else could see.

Endnotes

i.   https://www.inspiringquotes.us/author/9349-mae-jemison

ii.   Excerpt from letter from Mother Teresa to Archbishop Ferdinand Périer, 1953.

iii.   Quote from letter from Richard Hauptmann to Pauline Hauptmann. Translation from German to English by Trenton State Prison Staff. Dated December 27, 1935. Kept in Principal Keeper of the State Prison Colonel Mark O Kimberling's personal files until his death in 1964 thence in his wife's personal files until her death in 1977. http://www.lindberghkidnappinghoax.com/kim.pdf

iv.   Ibid.

v.   Ibid.

vi.   Ibid

vii.   Ibid.

viii.   Quotes from Jaroslav Nostersky. Examination by Lieutenant AT Keaten, Mr Frank Wilson and Sergeant A Zapolsky. 4 October 1934. New Jersey State Police Museum and Learning Centre Archives.

ix.   Ibid.

x. Ibid.

xi. Ibid.

xii. Ibid.

xiii. Quote from The Gay Science, Section 232. First published in 1882.